The Cowboy's Surprise Reunion

Cowboys of Whistle Rock Ranch, Book Five

Contemporary Western Romance

SHIRLEEN DAVIES

Books Series by Shirleen Davies

Historical Western Romances

Redemption Mountain
MacLarens of Fire Mountain Historical
MacLarens of Boundary Mountain

Romantic Suspense

Eternal Brethren Military Romantic Suspense
Peregrine Bay Romantic Suspense

Contemporary Western Romance

Cowboys of Whistle Rock Ranch
MacLarens of Fire Mountain Contemporary
Macklins of Whiskey Bend

The best way to stay in touch is to subscribe to my newsletter. Go to my Website *www.shirleendavies.com* and fill in your email and name in the
Join My Newsletter boxes. That's it!

Avalanche Ranch Press, LLC
PO Box 12618
Prescott, AZ 86304

The Cowboy's Surprise Reunion is a work of fiction. Names, characters, places, and incidents are either products of the author's imagination or used fictitiously. Any resemblance to actual events, locales, or persons, living or dead, is wholly coincidental.

Book design and conversions by Joseph Murray at 3rdplanetpublishing.com

Cover design by Sweet 'n Spicy Designs

ISBN: 978-1-947680-88-3

I care about quality, so if you find something in error, please contact me via email at **shirleen@shirleendavies.com**

Description

His selfish focus on a personal goal destroyed a once in a lifetime relationship. Could there still be hope for a second chance?

Quinn Sawyer thought he'd achieved his dream of breeding specialized beef at an Idaho ranch. Realizing it wasn't what he'd envisioned, Quinn now works for a ranch in Wyoming. The owner appreciates his skill working with Wagyu cattle, which produces meat consumers crave. Satisfied with his new job, he goes through each day with just one regret.

Abigail Kelman still can't forget the man who left her for his dream job. Deciding a change would do her good, she accepts a position as an assistant chef at a large ranch in southern Wyoming. Challenging and fulfilling, she tackles each day with a positive outlook. Until the day the man from her past appears in the ranch's dining room.

Neither is anxious to make the first move until events force them to face their shared past. Quinn wants to renew what they once had, while Abigail isn't as certain.

The appearance of a person Quinn knows nothing about stuns him. The implications are difficult to accept. The impact to his family uncertain.

Focusing on the unexpected change in his life, Quinn puts his efforts to renew his relationship on hold. When additional factors come to light, his priorities change. No matter the effect the stranger's appearance foretells, he needs Abbie in his life.

Will Quinn be able to accept the changes, allowing his relationship with Abbie to flourish? Or will he once again choose another course, leaving her behind for a second time?

The Cowboy's Surprise Reunion, book five in the Cowboys of Whistle Rock Ranch Contemporary Western Romance series, is a clean and wholesome, full-length novel with an HEA.

The Cowboy's Surprise Reunion

Prologue

Triple T Ranch
Idaho
November

Quinn Sawyer pulled free of the deep mud along the river's edge, tucking the young calf tight against his side. The rains hadn't let up for three days, causing massive flooding. Nothing had been spared, including barns and houses built in the lowlands.

Patience was in short supply as ranchers and their employees tried to cross waterways too deep for their vehicles. Abandoned trucks, SUVs, and cars dotted the countryside. It was a miracle there'd been no deaths.

Wrapping the calf in a heavy blanket, Quinn eased his truck into a low gear, making his way across the open pasture to the road twenty yards away. On the other side stood the mother. The fact she stayed away was curious.

"The water must've spooked her," Quinn mumbled. He reminded himself this amount of water would spook most animals.

Returning the calf to its mother, he turned toward the main ranch house. The weather was supposed to clear within hours. It would take days for the water to recede to normal levels, and the ranch hands to return to their regular chores.

Quinn had been at Triple T Ranch for two years, and he'd yet to experience anything similar to a standard cycle of work. The job had been explained as an incredible opportunity for a man with his education.

Perhaps if he'd been more mature, and less captivated by a position most would perceive as too good to be true, he would have turned them down. The incredible salary, and opportunity to put into practice what he'd learned in college, were too much to walk away from.

If he had said no, Quinn knew he would've always wondered. After all these months of dead ends and broken promises, he now couldn't stop thinking about what he'd left behind.

Who he'd left behind.

Parking in the driest spot he could find close to the barn, Quinn sloshed his way inside. The last setback had sealed his decision.

He'd been working with a breeding specialist to improve their line of Wagyu beef cattle. The problem wasn't in their methods, or the science behind the decisions. The problem was they were owned by a conglomerate made up of men and women who weren't ranchers. They had no bond with the land or the animals.

Their loyalties to projects lasted as long as the last big win. Monies and personnel shifted on the whims of the puppet masters back in Indianapolis. Quinn wished he'd known all of this sooner.

Entering his apartment at the far end of the barn, he stripped off his soggy clothes, and stepped into a hot shower. He'd identified this day as his last a month earlier, giving notice to his supervisor.

It had turned out to be an amicable parting. Quinn flew back to Indianapolis for an exit interview, stayed an extra day, then returned to Idaho to finish up his time.

Grabbing a towel, he dried off, shaved, and dressed. Firing up his laptop, he checked messages, a smile curving the corners of his mouth.

Quinn had been hoping for a response to an email he'd sent a week earlier. A good friend from college was the foreman at a well-known ranch in Wyoming. He'd tried to talk Quinn into taking a job there when they'd graduated, but he'd been determined to carve a future on his own.

Looking back, Quinn knew he'd been much too cocky and driven by pride. Being knocked down a couple notches since then had cured those ailments.

Reading the message a second time, Quinn answered the invitation to visit the ranch in Wyoming. All he had to do was pack a few items and get on the road.

Within a few hours, he'd be heading toward what he hoped would be a better future.

Chapter One

Kelman Ranch
March

Quinn Sawyer tugged the collar of his coat up, securing it from the frigid wind. A freak storm had hammered the area most of the night, building up already towering snowbanks.

Insistent wind woke him early, forcing his departure from the warm bed before four o'clock. Quinn made the rounds of the barn, stables, and corrals, satisfied all was as it should be.

He and three ranch hands had delivered hay to the herds before dinner the night before, checking water troughs on the way. They'd make another trip after lunch.

Quinn knew Jake and Beth Kelman would be rolling out of bed soon. Returning to the house, he fixed coffee, whipped up pancake batter, and pulled out a pound of bacon, along with a dozen eggs, from the refrigerator.

Sipping coffee, he thought about the day ahead. He was supposed to ride over to Whistle Rock Ranch with Jake after breakfast to make a decision on purchasing one of their stallions. It was a trip he'd been putting off for a while. Not because he didn't believe they needed the animal for their breeding program. His reasons for stalling had nothing to do with the horse, and everything to do with Beth's assistant in the Whistle Rock kitchen.

"Will you have time to head over to Whistle Rock with me?" Jake filled a cup with coffee before leaning against the counter and taking a sip.

"Plenty of time." Quinn topped off his cup before pouring the egg mixture into a frying pan. "The cattle and horses are fed. Our men can take care of everything else. Are you working in the kitchen today, Beth?"

"Lunch and dinner. Abigail is taking care of breakfast."

Quinn stilled at the mention of Abigail.

Jake's sister. The woman Quinn had left behind to take a job in Idaho. The same woman he'd avoided since taking the job at Kelman Ranch.

He didn't believe Abigail had recognized him from the one meal he'd taken at Whistle Rock. It had been a couple months earlier, on Jake and Beth's wedding day. There'd been a lot of people moving about. She'd been setting out appetizers, stopping long enough for her gaze to sweep the room. Her attention had moved right past him, nothing in her stance indicating recognition.

He'd been disappointed, then relieved. At the time, Quinn hadn't been ready to face the woman he'd left behind for an incredible opportunity in Idaho. His departure over two years ago had been sudden, allowing no time for him to explain himself.

Quinn had been certain the job was a way to make his mark in the highly competitive cattle breeding industry.

He'd thrown his clothes into a large satchel, loaded his horse into the trailer, and left.

Phone calls and texts to Abigail had gone unanswered. He'd written a three page letter, mailing it to the diner where she worked. It had been returned unopened. His attempts had continued for almost a year before realizing she wasn't going to respond.

Quinn hadn't blamed her. The split was on him. Any animosity she felt landed at his feet.

"Abigail wanted the day off," Beth continued. "I think she might be seeing someone."

Jake chewed his eggs, tilting his head in question.

"I think it might be the new doctor. He's the one Lily met in Sheridan when she and Virgil were figuring out if they had a future. I haven't met him, but Daisy says he's a real catch." She mentioned Wyatt Bonner's wife. The Bonners owned Whistle Rock Ranch.

Jake's brow arched. "A catch, huh?"

"According to Daisy. I'm glad for Abigail."

Rinsing his empty plate, he set it inside the dishwasher. "Why's that?"

"I'm pretty sure she's been a virtual recluse the last two years. She worked, but didn't do much socially. You're her brother, Jake. What do you think?"

"The same. She isn't the same outgoing sister I grew up with." He shrugged. "People change. I'm sure Abbie had her reasons for spending time alone." Grabbing his hat, Jake moved to the kitchen door. "You ready, Quinn?"

Jake's voice cut through his fogged brain. "Uh, yeah."

He'd tuned out when hearing Abigail might be seeing someone. Quinn shouldn't have been surprised. Abigail was a beautiful woman with a warm personality and magnificent smile.

When they'd been a couple, he'd been proud to be seen with her. Acknowledging he never should've left for Idaho without speaking to her still chafed. Was he jealous she might be seeing another man? Absolutely. Was he prepared to do something about it?

"No." He hadn't meant to say it out loud.

Beth glanced at him. "Did you say something, Quinn?"

"What? Uh, no. Are you riding over with us?"

She shook her head. "I'm going in my truck. See you there." Beth headed back upstairs as Quinn followed Jake outside.

"I'm not locked into buying the stallion." Jake climbed into his truck, waiting to turn the engine until Quinn joined him. "I believe he'd be a good addition."

"Did Wyatt approach you about buying him?"

"Both him and Virgil. They have enough for their needs. This one was born on the ranch, has great bloodlines, and the potential for large stud fees."

"Has he sired any foals?"

"Four. All are doing well. Each will bring the Bonners big money."

Quinn didn't respond, his mind moving to Abigail. "How does your sister like working at the ranch?"

"Loves it. She and Beth get along great."

Drop it, Quinn told himself. He didn't want Jake to know what a fool he'd been to let Abigail go. Instead, he moved the subject to a much safer topic.

"I have some ideas about introducing Wagyu cattle to the ranch. There's an operation in Idaho who'd be willing to help us get started."

"I've been meaning to talk to you about that. We have a good business with the prime Angus beef, but the future requires us to expand. Wagyu beef is the most logical." Jake turned into Whistle Rock Ranch. Parking, he turned toward Quinn. "What would be the best way to connect with this rancher?"

"I'll call him. We should consider driving up to see his operation. It's impressive."

Climbing out of the truck, Jake led the way to the corral where the stallion would be waiting. "Set it up and I'll make it work."

Abigail Kelman watched her brother, Jake, and his foreman out of the kitchen window, stomach clenching. Quinn Sawyer hadn't set foot on Whistle Rock Ranch since Beth and Jake's wedding.

It had been a shock to see the man who'd talked of marriage at the ranch. She and Quinn had been close. Close enough to discuss a shared future, marriage, and children.

They'd spent all their free time together. At one point, Abigail thought she knew him as well as she knew herself. How wrong she'd been.

It had taken a long time for her to come to terms with his disappearance. She'd read his emails and texts, but never responded. A letter had arrived, but she'd refused delivery. Abigail believed she deserved to hear his explanation in person. By the time a year had passed, and his attempts to contact her stopped, she knew he had no plans to return.

Abigail had heard the story of how Quinn arrived at the ranch. He and Virgil had been friends in college, staying in contact after graduation. Quinn left a job in Idaho to accept Jake's offer to become his foreman. Little had been said about his time before moving to Idaho. No one knew she was a part of his past.

"Thanks for taking care of breakfast." Beth tied an apron around her waist. "I thought you were taking the day off, Abbie."

"I wanted to wait until you showed up. The filling for the lunch enchiladas is made and in the refrigerator. Same with the sauce. You wanted brisket for dinner, so I defrosted two large ones. They're marinating."

"That's more than I expected." Beth studied Abigail.

Smiles were a rare occurrence for her assistant. She'd been tempted to ask about her past several times since she came to Whistle Rock, but always shoved aside her curiosity. If Abigail wanted to confide in her, she would.

Still, she wished there was a way to elicit a smile. Even a small one.

"Have you met Jake's foreman?"

Slipping a strand of hair behind an ear, Abigail took several steps away from the window and her view of Quinn.

"Not yet. There's plenty of time. I'm sure he'll be staying a while." Hanging her apron on a hook, she glanced around the kitchen. "I need to get going if I'm going to meet Mason at the coffee and bakery shop." She had to get out of there before Beth decided to introduce her to Quinn.

"What are your plans?"

"I'm not sure. Mason had some ideas, which is good with me. We could take a walk around town and I'd be happy."

"Easy to please, huh?"

Abigail stopped by the back door with her hand on the knob. "Maybe I am."

"Well, have a wonderful time. I'll see you in the morning."

Taking a quick look outside, assuring herself Quinn wouldn't see her, she took the longer path to where everyone parked their vehicles.

Abigail's spirits lifted when her gaze landed on her new wheels.

She'd been able to save enough to purchase a used Jeep. It had been parked in an empty lot with For Sale signs taped to several windows. Abigail had been riding into town with Jake and asked him to look at it.

It was white with no visible damage. The price listed was a little high, but she figured the owner might be willing to budge a little.

Jotting down the number, she left a message, then another one the following day. Deciding the owner had sold the Jeep to someone else, she'd put it out of her mind.

A week later, she got a return call. After a brief conversation, she agreed to meet the owner in town the following afternoon.

Lily, Virgil Redstar's wife, was heading to town and took Abigail with her. They waited almost an hour for the owner to arrive before climbing back into Lily's car.

"I'll call him to reschedule. Sorry you wasted all this time waiting with me."

"It's fine, Abbie. It sure is a fine looking Jeep. I wonder why he's selling it."

The words had barely left her mouth when a gray pickup turned into the lot and parked. A man jumped out.

"Sorry. I got held up," he said before his gaze lit on Lily.

"Mason? Are you the Jeep's owner?"

"Sure am."

From there, it wasn't long before Mason and Abigail agreed on a price. Taking her down payment, he handed her the keys. Before she drove off, he'd gotten her to agree to a date.

"And today's the day," she mumbled, climbing into the Jeep and driving off.

Chapter Two

Quinn stood next to the barn, watching Abigail dash to a white Jeep, climb inside, and drive off. On the way to her date, he figured.

Funny how, for the last couple years, he hadn't allowed himself to think about her going out with other men. It was different now. Today, the fact she'd be spending the day with another man ate at him.

Quinn knew he had no right to feel anything about her choice to date someone else. He'd been the one to walk away in a manner guaranteed to ruin any future with Abigail. Some decisions couldn't be reversed.

"We're all set, Quinn. You'll load the stallion into one of the Bonner trailers, transport him to my ranch, then return the trailer."

"You made a good decision, boss. The stallion is a fine animal."

"He'll be the foundation of the horse breeding program. I have to get going. Virgil is sending one of their ranch hands over to help. You can do it alone, but I'm not going to turn down help." Jake jogged back toward where Virgil and Wyatt worked with a few of the men.

"Hey. Are you Quinn?"

"I am."

"Great. I'm Sam. Virgil sent me over to help you with the stallion."

He hoped the shock didn't show on his face. Sam was about five-feet-four with short black hair and warm brown eyes. It was her curves that stalled his thinking.

"That's uh, great."

She chuckled at his attempt to hide his surprise. "I've been working with horses my entire life. This one is a terrific animal. I'm amazed they're selling him." She glanced over her shoulder to where the stallion stood in a turnout. "Well, you ready to load him?"

"Uh...yes."

"I'll grab his halter. We're going to use the three-horse trailer. He loads and unloads real well with it. Heck, it might be easier to tack him up and ride him to Jake's place. Then we'd have to haul the saddle and tack back here. Oh, well. The trailer it is."

Sam seemed to bounce away, radiating energy with every step. Her positive attitude was infectious. A grin turned up the corners of Quinn's mouth. He already felt better than before she introduced herself.

Working together, they loaded the stallion without incident. Sam asked questions about Jake's ranch and Quinn's job on the way to the Kelman place. It never felt as if she were prying. She just seemed interested in everything.

He'd never met anyone like Sam, and he found himself wondering if she was dating anyone. The instant the thought popped into his head, he shoved it aside. Her personal life wasn't his business.

"Do you already have mares?" Sam sat up straighter as they entered the area around the ranch house and barns.

"Two, with a possible third mare Jake may purchase from a rancher at the south end of town."

"Then you'll be concentrating on quarter horses?"

"That's the plan for now. Sam, would you mind getting out and directing me toward the stall at the far left?"

"You got it." Jumping to the ground, she ran around behind the trailer. Using hand signals, she had him in position with one try. "Perfect!" Two thumbs in the air punctuated her shout.

The stallion gave them no problem when exiting the trailer. Entering the stall was something else. He didn't want to enter his new home. Twice as big as the other stalls, with a large outside pen, it had an oversized feed door and manger, heated waterer, and tack closet. No matter how enticing it might be, the stallion refused to step inside.

"I have an idea." Sam took the lead line from Quinn. "I'm going to take him around back to the gate for the outside pen. I'll guide him inside, remove the halter and line, then leave him alone. The door between the pen and stall is already open. It may take a little time, but he'll eventually go into the stall."

"Great idea, Sam."

And it was. Within ten minutes, the stallion had ventured into the stall, tried the waterer, and filled his mouth with loose hay.

"That went well." Quinn watched through the bars as the horse walked around, snorted a couple times, then continued to get settled. "I'd better get you back to Whistle Rock."

"You don't have to drive back. I'm good going on my own. I've driven with a trailer hundreds of times."

Waving as Sam pulled away, Quinn felt a twinge of something he couldn't define. He didn't believe it had to do with the spirited ranch hand. She was interesting and animated.

Sam would make a great friend. Anything more? Quinn didn't think so. At least not for him.

Abigail gripped the panic bar inside Mason's truck as he took another turn on the frozen trail. He wasn't driving fast. It was the ice which made it exciting if a little scary.

They were meeting a real estate agent to look at three cabins in the local mountains. All were vacant and priced to sell.

"I hope this is all right, Abbie. It hadn't been my plan to visit properties on our first date." Mason made another turn, keeping within twenty feet of his agent's four-wheeler.

"This is great. I hardly ever take time to get off the ranch. Seeing cabins is a bonus. Did you have a place in Sheridan?"

Maneuvering a tight curve, he straightened the truck. "Four bedrooms, a den, and an office for a single man. Ridiculous. I won't go that big here."

She smiled. The largest house she and her brother, Jake, had lived in was three bedrooms. No den, no office, and one bathroom. But that was all right. It taught them time management and how to share.

"Looks like we're at the first cabin."

Cabin? Abigail thought the place looked more like a mansion. "It's pretty big."

"Yeah. We're starting with the largest, which is five bedrooms. I don't know why I let the agent talk me into seeing it." Parking, he hurried around the truck to open Abigail's door. Holding out his hand, he helped her to the ground.

"This is pretty exciting. I've never looked for a place to buy."

"Then this will be a good experience for you." He didn't release her hand as they took the path to the front porch steps.

The tour of the three story house took almost half an hour. Whoever built it put a lot of money into the construction and furnishings.

"The second place isn't too far away. Is this too boring for you?"

She shook her head. "Not at all. It's much better than the laundry I'd be doing if I were at the ranch."

The next house didn't interest Mason. It was the third cabin that caught his attention. Three bedrooms, three baths, a great kitchen, and an incredible view to the Tetons sold the place. He made an offer, then put it out of his mind while they ate an early dinner at the steakhouse in Brilliance.

"How do you like working at the ranch?"

"It's great. Beth is a wonderful boss, and you don't get much better than the Bonners. I'm able to try different recipes, which never happened at the diner in Sheridan."

"That's right. You're from Sheridan."

"Yep. Jake called me about the need for a chef's assistant." She chuckled. "I didn't have to think about it for more than a minute. What made you decide to take the job at the hospital?"

"Lily called me about it. We met when she drove to Sheridan for a job interview. I'd finally been cleared to work after a pretty devastating accident. Brilliance seemed to be a good change for me."

"An accident?"

"Hit and run. Broke my legs, plus other injuries. Took a long time to get myself back together." He sipped his beer before continuing. "Lots of physical therapy. The hospital held my job for me, but Lily's call came before I started back."

"How are you enjoying Brilliance?"

"It's great. Wonderful people, and the job is perfect. I grab coffee every morning at Brilliance Coffee & Bakery. Lydia is a real nice lady. Her scones are the best I've ever eaten."

"Beth sometimes goes into town just to buy Lydia' pastries. She'll come back with four dozen. The chocolat croissants are incredible. Someday, I'd like to try my hand at creating pastries."

"You should talk to Lydia about apprenticing unde her." Taking the last bite of his steak, Mason slid the plate away. "She might be able to work around your schedule a the ranch."

"I've thought about it. Right now, I can't fit a second job into my schedule. It's a good dream, though." Finishing the last of her soda, she leaned back in her chair as Mason's phone rang.

"Mason Nagle. That's great. Do I need to come by tonight or is tomorrow after my shift soon enough? Perfect I'll see you then." Ending the call, he slid his phone into a pocket. "They accepted my offer. Looks like I'll be a homeowner again."

"Congratulations! That's wonderful news."

"Yeah, it is."

"You don't sound too excited."

"Buying a place and moving in takes a lot of time. I sold all my furniture with the house in Sheridan."

"So, you'll need to shop."

Chuckling, he picked up the glass of water and took a long swallow. "Not my favorite thing to do on a day off."

"Let me know if you want some help. Except, well...it might be hard to match schedules." She thought of the few hours a week available for personal time. "Beth might be open to giving me a day or two off."

"It's all right, Abbie. I can make it work. Would you like dessert?"

"Thanks, but I can't eat another bite."

"I'll get you back to your car."

They spoke little on the short drive from the steakhouse to where she parked. Abigail liked Mason, enjoyed their time looking at cabins.

"How about dinner on Saturday, Abbie? I heard the Italian place is pretty good."

"I've heard the same. I'd love to have dinner."

Thanking her for a wonderful time, Mason waited until she climbed into her car before jogging back to his truck.

Driving to the ranch, Abigail thought about seeing him again on Saturday. The expected excitement didn't come. Concentrating on the road, she didn't worry too much about her lack of enthusiasm. By Saturday, she'd be more than ready for dinner with Mason.

Turning into the ranch, she found a spot and parked, but didn't leave the car.

Her mind traveled to Quinn. It had been more than two years since he'd left, and she still missed him every day.

Though he lived less than one mile away, it might as well have been a thousand.

Chapter Three

Jonah Bonner reviewed the numbers for a third time, frowning as he had twice before. There had to be an error somewhere in the spreadsheet. But where?

As chief financial officer and legal counsel for Whistle Rock Ranch, Jonah prided himself on being thorough and meticulous. The decisions made using his documentation demanded perfection, and he was used to delivering it.

Winter would soon give way to spring, ushering in a new season of dude ranch guests. Which was the reason he'd locked himself into the office to complete the financial forecasts. But the numbers weren't adding up.

Even with the expenses associated with the addition of several more cabins and expanding the season, he was showing a larger net income than his previous projections.

Scrubbing a hand down his face, Jonah grabbed a bottle of water, swallowing half of it. Maybe he should take a break. It had been at least a week since he'd traded in his khaki pants and lightweight shirt for warmer clothes, tacking up his horse for a long ride.

Making up his mind, he walked to the office next to his. Knocking, he shoved the door open. His younger brother, Gage, held the phone to his ear, listening to whoever was on the other end.

Jonah walked to the window, looking out at the cabins, corrals, and barns. With the snow still several inches deep, most of the ranch hands were busying themselves around the main compound.

"I'll call you next week." Gage set his phone on the desk. "What's up, Jonah?"

"I need to get out of here. Feel like taking a ride?"

"Excellent. Let me change clothes and I'll meet you in the barn."

Jonah was tacking up his horse when Gage joined him. They were mounted and riding out of the barn within fifteen minutes. Jonah fell in step alongside Gage.

"Which way?" Jonah asked.

"Let's ride north. There are some trails I want to check out." In charge of the adventure activities, Gage worked hard to keep up on the changes around the ranch.

"North it is."

They rode for almost an hour, Jonah feeling the stress melt away the farther from the ranch house they got. It had been this way since he was a boy. When he and his father disagreed, all he had to do was jump on his horse and ride.

Today had nothing to do with Anson Bonner, and everything to do with numbers. He was sure within minutes of returning to the office he'd find the error and correct the net profit.

"What magic are you adding to the schedule this year, Gage?"

"No magic, but I am adding longer ziplines. Seems a majority of our guests have done it before and would like more of a challenge."

"More liability?" Jonah also handled all the insurance for the ranch.

"Not really. Longer doesn't mean more dangerous. I've already spoken with Jake about extending the last landing by about a hundred yards. The guests will actually land six feet above the ground rather than about fifty. Fewer stairs at the end when they're already tired and their legs are spindly." Gage smiled on the last.

"I think we should try it out, make sure there are no problems."

"You can count on it."

"What else are you planning?"

"I've been given permission to use Big Lake for kayaking in early June. It took months to get the permit. It finally arrived last week. We can start right away instead of waiting until early July."

"Fishing?"

"The guests can fish from the shore or off the kayak. I have to figure that part out, as it's a little tricky. A lot will depend on the guest's fishing experience."

"Anything else?"

"I've arranged some tours not available last year. We'll also be offering more horseback rides. They were real popular last season. Same with ranch rodeos. We only had a couple last season. I'm looking at doubling or tripling that number. It helped that Trace was a champion rodeo contestant."

"Jake competed, right?" Jonah asked.

"He did, and won several championships. We'll push that in our marketing material."

"If you're done checking trails, I should head back."

Reining their horses around, they took their time, unaware of the man watching them through binoculars.

Blake Nielsen, one of the newer ranch hands, reached into the toolbox, holding out the pliers Owen needed. They worked together, tightening the smooth fence wire.

Owen Baker had been with Whistle Rock Ranch for a while. Married with two kids, he'd taken the job a few months after being released from prison for attempting to steal painkillers for his wife.

It had been his only offense. Unfortunately, getting hired with any record had proven difficult. The Bonners were glad to have him. They felt the same about Blake. He'd been in prison for less than a year before being released when his conviction was overturned.

"I heard you've had experience working on cars." Owen tightened the wire, wrapping and tying it off. "Ever worked on ranch equipment?"

"When I was inside." Blake referred to his time in prison. "We worked on all kinds of vehicles and equipment. I seem to have a talent for fixing stuff."

"Have you mentioned your skills to Virgil?"

"I may have said something about working on cars."

"Might want to think about letting him and Wyatt know."

"Good idea." Blake grabbed another roll of wire.

"The more you can do, the better your chance of not getting laid off when work slows in the fall."

Owen wasn't a man who wasted words. It hadn't taken Blake long to learn when the man did speak, it was wise to listen.

"I'll talk to Virgil later today. Thanks."

Blake knew he'd been lucky to land this job. There were other, more experienced, men looking for work. He'd be a fool not to do everything possible to hang on.

The one dark cloud hovering over him was miles away in another state, with no idea where Blake had landed. If he could keep his location a mystery, it would make both their lives so much better.

Aiden Winters tucked his binoculars in the case, his heart racing with anticipation. He'd been tracking down his bounty for two months. Never had he experienced a hunt this difficult, and he was eager to close it out. All the evidence he needed was tucked into a folio—a document that had been signed in the dead of night a week ago, proving beyond a doubt the wanted man worked here at the ranch. Climbing into his truck, his mind raced with what to do next.

At six-foot-two, Aiden Winters was a rugged, scarred, bounty hunter, with a muscular build from years of physical training and fighting. His long, dark hair fell in unruly locks around his shoulders, while his piercing blue eyes constantly scanned his surroundings, always alert for any possible threats.

He reminded himself this wasn't a typical hunt, and arresting his target would be difficult. The Bonners were a well-respected ranching family with strong ties to the area. His usual approach wouldn't work. He couldn't charge in and take the man by force.

This would have to be a negotiated arrest. The Bonners deserved to know his plan in advance. They'd have to trust him and back away when the takedown took place. His gut told him it would be a hard sell. The Bonners were a loyal bunch and wouldn't give up one of their men easily.

Starting the engine, he followed the narrow road back to the highway. This was going to take more thought. His target wasn't going anywhere soon.

He almost felt sorry for the man. All he wanted was to start over, put the mistake behind him, and create a new life.

If Aiden did his job right, the target would have a new life. Just not the one he anticipated.

Quinn threw the ball toward the barn, smiling as Duke ran after it. Dropping it next to Quinn's booted feet, he waited until it flew through the air again.

Jake had rescued the golden Labrador retriever from a pack of wild dogs a few months earlier. When posting flyers and paying for ads in the local paper hadn't turned up an owner, Jake adopted him.

He'd become the perfect ranch dog. Horses and steers didn't intimidate him. Duke was patient, attentive, and possibly the smartest dog Quinn had ever known.

A dozen throws later, Quinn sucked down a bottle of water and left to visit the stallion. He had to admit Lazarus was magnificent.

The quarter horse's coat was a roan color, with a mix of white and black hairs creating a blue appearance. When the sun shone on the stallion, his coat was a beautiful blue velvet.

Watching him gallop around the large corral, Quinn's first thought was of a fierce warrior, proud, strong, willing to do whatever was necessary to keep his kingdom safe. Quinn had the privilege of watching this warrior.

"Amazing, isn't he?"

Quinn stiffened at Jake's voice, then relaxed. "I didn't hear you come up."

"Like most everyone else, you were mesmerized by the stallion." Jake rested his arms on the top rung of the fence, his gaze fixed on the horse. "I didn't buy him."

"What?"

"In the end, Wyatt and I decided we'd both use Lazarus at stud."

Quinn watched the stallion before nodding. "Good decision. I assume you'll pay a stud fee."

"Yes. We threw out numbers, but didn't decide on anything. I'm sure Wyatt will be fair. You'll manage the breeding schedule with our mares, as I'll be busy at Whistle Rock. Any issues with that?"

"Not at all. It's what I did in Idaho. Horse breeding was much smaller than their cattle business. I spent a great deal of time with the company scientists to increase the production and quality of the meat. They were Angus, though we'd added Wagyu a few months before I left."

Jake turned toward Quinn. "That's the direction we're going. Improve our Angus cattle and add Wagyu. We'll concentrate on what we have the first year while we ascertain the demand for Wagyu in the northwest states. I've been working with Beth to draw up a marketing plan. She knows the restaurants who'd have the money to invest in high quality beef."

A truck coming toward the house caught their attention. Jake frowned before walking to where the truck stopped. Beth and Abigail sat inside. Odd, in that both were supposed to be working in the kitchen at Whistle Rock.

"What's going on?"

Beth climbed out. "Margie and Monica forgot to tell us they'd hired Lydia from Brilliance Coffee & Bakery to bring lunch for the ranch hands today. She's testing out adding sandwiches, paninis, soup, and salad to the menu." She flipped strands of hair off her face. "Abigail and I wrapped up the lasagna, spaghetti, sauces, and bread." She smiled. "We brought enough of everything for us to have lunch."

Abigail made her way around the truck to stand next to Beth. She had a hard time keeping her gaze on the ground instead of on Quinn. Jake waved for him to join them.

"You've met Quinn, right, Abbie?" Beth asked.

"Um..." Before she could finish, Quinn stopped a few feet away.

"Abbie and I have met, but it's been a long time."

"Not long enough," she muttered, then covered her mouth with a hand. It wasn't fast enough for the others not to hear. "We knew each other in Sheridan."

"It's good to see you." Walking to her, Quinn bent to kiss her cheek, but she stepped away.

"Look, I'm not hungry, and I have some errands to run before we fix dinner. Thanks for the invitation, Beth."

Before anyone realized her intent, she'd rushed around the truck to walk back to Whistle Rock.

Quinn blew out a breath. "I'll take her back."

"No, you won't," Abigail yelled over her shoulder, picking up her pace.

"Stubborn woman."

"I'll help Beth bring in the food for lunch if you'll drive Abbie back to the ranch. Then, I want to hear about you two, and what's got her so fired up."

Chapter Four

Abigail drew her coat around her while avoiding patches of melted snow and mud. At least she'd worn her old rubber boots.

This was not how she'd wanted to face Quinn after more than two years. It had been a miracle they hadn't run into each other sooner. Spotting him across the room at Jake and Beth's didn't count, as Abigail was certain Quinn hadn't recognized her.

Seeing him today, being close enough to touch him brought back all the memories she'd tried so hard to forget. She'd been surprised when he offered to drive her back to Whistle Rock.

Increasing her pace, her gaze landed on the small barn at the ranch. Not much longer before she'd be back in the kitchen and wouldn't have to deal with Quinn Sawyer.

The sound of an engine had her spine stiffening. Instinctively, she moved to the side of the road, hoping the vehicle would pass. Her hope vanished when it slowed to match her speed.

"Please get in the truck, Abbie."

She waved a hand in the air. "I'm almost there." Stumbling, she landed in a muddy rut. To her irritation, it sucked in her left boot. "Rats."

Abigail didn't have time to pull her foot out before she was swept up in Quinn's arms. A strangled yelp burst from her throat as her arms flailed.

"Put me down."

"I plan to." Walking around the truck, he deposited her on the passenger seat. "I'll get your boot."

With one boot still stuck in the mud, she couldn't get out of the truck and walk. All Abigail could do was silently fume at the way her attempt at walking back to the ranch had backfired.

"Here you are. Come on, Abbie, slip your foot into it." Quinn held the boot out.

Resisting would do no good and only prolong their time together. "Fine." She slid her foot into the boot, crossed her arms, and stared out the windshield.

Driving the rest of the way, Quinn took a few furtive glances at her before attempting conversation.

"You look good, Abbie. As if you're happy with everything." Lame, he thought, but gritted his teeth instead of rewording his ridiculous attempts to break the ice.

She glared at him before returning her attention to the front.

"Jake says Beth loves working with you."

The frigid atmosphere of the truck's interior continued as they rounded the bend before turning into Whistle Rock Ranch.

"Would you be available for dinner sometime soon?" Stopping in the expansive parking area, he didn't have time to say anything more before she opened the door and got out.

"Thank you for the ride." Slamming the door harder than necessary, she made her way between vehicles to the kitchen door.

"That went well," he muttered before putting the truck in reverse and heading back to Kelman Ranch.

The short drive didn't give him much time to reflect on what else he could've said to Abigail. Maybe the wise choice would've been to stay silent. That seemed ridiculous when there was less than two feet separating them.

He'd wanted to reach out and cover her hand with his, knowing the gesture would be rejected. Now he had to face Jake, and probably Beth. They deserved an explanation, even if it cast him in a terrible light.

Parking the truck, he headed up the steps to the front door. Two raps and Jake yelled for him to come in. He found them in the kitchen with food spread out on the counter.

Beth handed him a plate. "There's plenty, so don't be shy."

Quinn loaded up with lasagna, spaghetti, and bread, taking a seat at the kitchen table. Jake and Beth did the same, joining him. They ate in silence for several minutes before Jake spoke.

"You and Abbie knew each other back in Sheridan?"

Setting down his fork, Quinn swallowed some water. "We met at the diner where Abbie worked. I was working at a nearby ranch. The owner wanted to add Wagyu beef to the mix. He never took the leap. During my time there, I'd go to the diner as often as possible. Abbie and I became close, even talked of marriage, having a family."

Jake's brows drew together in a severe frown, though he stayed silent.

"I'm the one who messed everything up."

"Figured as much from the way Abbie acted," Jake said. "How did you mess it all up, Quinn?"

He saw the concern on Beth's face and wished he could ignore his failings. "When I realized my boss wasn't going to go forward with expansion, I started exploring other options. Abbie and I talked about the likelihood of me having to relocate. She had no desire to leave Sheridan. Wouldn't even discuss it."

Shoving his plate away, he grabbed another bottle of water from the counter, drinking half of it. Retaking his seat, he set the half full bottle on the table.

"A letter came for me about a month into my job search. It was from a big conglomerate in Indiana. They own businesses in the agricultural space and wanted to expand into ranch operations. Just before contacting me, they bought two large cattle operations in the Northwest. They wanted to hire me to introduce Wagyu beef into their line of brands. Actually, they hired more than twenty people to expand. The opportunity was incredible for someone at my level." He chuckled. "Meaning, I was at the bottom of that particular food chain. I went through several interviews in Idaho and Indiana. I didn't hear from them for several weeks, then an offer arrived. They gave me a day to decide. Three days to arrive at the ranch in Idaho."

"You accepted." Beth offered a small smile.

"I did. Abbie was out of town with friends for a few days, and didn't answer her phone. I left a message, packed, and drove to Idaho. She didn't call me back. I continued to call, sent emails, texts, and finally wrote a letter. Abbie didn't respond to any of my attempts."

"Guess she was serious about not leaving Sheridan." Jake shook his head. "That's Abigail. Stubborn all the way."

"She didn't try to contact you during your entire time in Idaho?" Beth asked.

"Not once." He ran a hand over his face. "I saw Abbie at your wedding, but didn't approach her. She'd changed her hair, but I still recognized her. It was the eyes." Rising, he rinsed his plate and utensils, placing them in the dishwasher.

"Did she say anything when you took her back to the ranch?"

He looked at Beth, shaking his head. "She thanked me. That was it."

"At least she didn't bite your head off," Jake said. "My older sister has a pretty sharp temper."

Quinn smiled. "Yeah, I've witnessed it. Just once, but it was enough."

Jake shoved his chair back and stood. "What are your plans regarding her?"

"Other than trying to get her to talk to me, I don't have any. From what I've heard, she's dating some doctor in

town. Sounds corny, but I just want her to be happy."
Opening the back door, he paused. "I'd better get going.
Don't want to waste what daylight is left."

Abigail removed pans from cupboards, slamming them
onto the counter. Cringing, she was glad Beth wasn't
around to see her meltdown.

She hadn't been able to shake off her sour mood since
Quinn had driven away. The bulk of the problem came from
her own sense of guilt at never responding to any of his
attempts to talk.

Anger at his leaving, then pride, had kept her from
returning his calls or messages. A month, then two, then
three months went by, and just like that, he'd been gone a
year. She'd been certain he'd return, try to convince her to
leave Sheridan for Idaho. But he never did.

Instead, he'd persisted in trying to get her to respond
to him. She'd dug in her heels. More than two years later,
Abigail knew most of the blame for their breakup fell on
her. All because she couldn't talk him into staying in
Sheridan.

"In a boring job where he'd be miserable," she
muttered.

Setting both hands on the edge of the counter, she let
out a shaky breath. She thought her love of Sheridan would

keep her there forever. It was what she told Quinn, what she believed about herself.

Yet here she was, in Brilliance. A couple hundred miles from a home she promised to never leave. Was it a coincidence Quinn was here, also?

"Hey. Sorry I'm late." Beth slipped into an apron, tying it at the waist. "Have you started anything?"

Plastering on the best smile she could, Abigail motioned toward the roaster. "The chickens are roasting. The vegetables are ready to cook. I haven't started the risotto or the bread, but the desserts are ready. Hope everyone's hungry tonight."

"I'm sure they will be. Have you heard anything about the lunch from Brilliance Coffee & Bakery?"

"No one's come into the kitchen since I returned an hour ago. I can't imagine the men complaining. Everyone loves Lydia's cooking."

"It was a test to see how expanding her menu would go over. I sure hope it went well. Okay. We have two hours. What's up first, Abbie?"

"Oh, I'm so glad both of you are here." Margie Bonner blew into the kitchen, a broad smile fixed on her face. "I wanted both of you to know the lunch was a huge success. The ranch hands ate every crumb and drop of soup. Nothing was left, including the desserts. Lydia is going to start with two different paninis, her chicken salad sandwich, and a roast beef and ham sandwich. Afterall, this is ranch country."

"That's wonderful news," Beth said. "How did they like the soups?"

Margie lifted her hands in the air. "They loved them. Lydia will start with two on the menu and rotate two different ones every week. It simply could not have gone better. What smells so good in here?"

"Abbie is roasting chickens for dinner. She has this special rub everyone likes. Something similar is used for the vegetables. I'm assuming you, Anson, and the rest of the Bonners will be here."

"Plus Virgil and Lily. His parents are eating in town tonight. I still have a few things to finish up before dinner. Just wanted you ladies to know lunch was a success." They watched her leave.

Eyes wide, Abigail's mouth curved into a grin. "She always reminds me of a tornado, or a hurricane. Or an earthquake, depending on what's happening."

"She does have endless energy. All right. Let's get back to dinner."

Abigail was glad for the interruption, and the positive force Margie left behind. It was what she needed to keep her mind off Quinn. At least long enough to get dinner on the table.

Chapter Five

Abigail took another glance in the mirror before grabbing her coat. The black slacks fit her perfectly, as did the pink, long sleeved sweater. The black leather boots made her legs look long and lean.

Hesitating, she set down the coat. Opening a drawer, she rifled through the contents, pulling out a pink, black, and cream scarf. She wrapped it around her neck twice before finishing the loose knot.

"Better." Picking up the coat and crossbody purse, Abigail left her living quarters behind the kitchen, stopping in the kitchen to speak with Beth. "You sure you don't need my help for dinner tonight?"

"Everything's covered. Do you know where Mason's taking you?"

"He mentioned an Italian restaurant. Any place would be fine. Oh, and you know he bought a house, right?"

Beth nodded as she took another serving bowl from a cupboard. "You told me after you spent the day looking at homes with him."

Abigail touched her forehead, grimacing. "Oh, that's right. I don't know how I forgot. Anyway, Mason sold all his furniture with his place in Sheridan. I offered to help him select new items, but I may need a day off. Any problem with that?"

"None at all. Give me at least a few days' notice." Glancing at the clock on the wall, she turned the oven heat to low. "So...you and Quinn knew each other before you took this job." Beth's soft gaze met Abigail's.

"We met in the diner where I worked in Sheridan. I thought he was real cute."

Beth smiled. "Guess I never thought of him as cute."

Her cheeks flushed. "You're right. My opinion moved from cute to amazingly handsome by the time he'd come in the third time. He came for lunch two or three times a week, and dinner once or twice. It took a while, but he asked me out after a few weeks. We spent a lot of time together after the first date."

"What happened?"

"He accepted a job in Idaho and left." Abigail bit her bottom lip while staring at the ground. "It was complicated."

"Ah." Beth gave a slow nod. "Most relationships are."

"I could've handled his move better. He wanted me to come out after he got settled. Said he'd find me an apartment not far from the ranch."

"But?"

"I wasn't ready to leave Sheridan." Checking the time, Abigail inched toward the door. "I'd better leave. I'm meeting Mason at the restaurant. Thanks again, Beth."

"No problem. Have a good time."

Abigail zipped up her coat as she hurried to the car and slid inside. She tried and failed to keep from looking toward the lights coming from Jake and Beth's ranch. Somewhere below those lights, Quinn was finishing his day.

Pulling onto the highway, she gripped the steering wheel tighter than needed. Abigail told herself it was because of the remnants of the last snowstorm on the road. It was a lie. She'd experienced tremors since sharing the truck with Quinn earlier that day.

The simplest solution would be to force him from her thoughts, replacing him with someone else. Mason would do well.

She guessed him to be a couple inches over six feet. Smart, with an excellent job, he was handsome in a different way than Quinn. Where Quinn was rugged looking with muscles from working on the ranch, Mason was good-looking in a citified way.

Where Quinn wore jeans, flannel or chambray work shirts, and boots, Mason preferred khaki slacks, button-down shirts, and loafers. Abigail thought for a moment, realizing she'd never seen Quinn in anything but jeans and boots.

She parked in the lot adjacent to the restaurant, staying in the car several minutes longer than necessary. The hesitancy had little to do with Mason.

Reconnecting with Quinn sat heavy on her heart. Being so close triggered old feelings to surface, forcing Abigail to face her part in their breakup.

It was uncomfortable to accept how immature and selfish her reaction to him leaving Idaho had been. There'd been nights when sleep refused to come, her thoughts consumed with regret. By morning, she always seemed to rationalize her decisions, refusing to contact Quinn.

Considering her life now, how she'd left Sheridan for the job at Whistle Rock Ranch, Abigail wished she'd gone to Idaho.

Mason stood inside the restaurant, coat slung over his arm. A smile broke across his face when he spotted Abigail through the glass entry door.

"Good evening."

"Sorry I'm late." Shrugging out of her coat, she handed it to Mason, who passed both off to the hostess.

"You are right on time. They have a table ready for us."

"Wonderful. I'm starving." She wasn't, but Abigail was determined to enjoy the evening.

Monday arrived too soon. Not that the weekend was any different than weekdays for Quinn. He worked seven days, appreciating the opportunity to stay busy.

Today would be a little different. Quinn's contact, an expert in the marketing of Wagyu beef to restaurants, would be arriving before lunch.

He'd met Benny Takada while at the University of Wyoming. Born in the United States, Takada had spent considerable time in Japan, learning the customs. During one particular summer, he'd spent two months with an uncle who possessed deep knowledge of Wagyu beef.

41

Interested in the potential for expanding sales of the meat in the United States, he'd been allowed to spend longer periods of time with his uncle while on vacation from his university studies. He and Quinn had met during Takada's senior year, forming an instant friendship.

"Morning, Quinn."

He turned to see Jake coming down the steps. "Good morning. Beth already gone?"

"She left a couple hours ago. It's makes for long days, but she loves it. When is your Wagyu specialist arriving?" Jake looked past Quinn to the cattle grazing in a nearby pasture.

"Should be anytime. I haven't seen Benny in a while. Knowing him, he'll have a full marketing plan for us to see."

"Without talking to us?"

Quinn chuckled. "He'd already done a few hours of research on the area. That, plus what I gave him, is more than he'll need to sketch something out for us."

"That him?" Jake nodded toward the road in and out of the ranch.

A deep blue Chevrolet four-wheel drive truck came toward them, Benny parking in the open area near the barn. Climbing out, he held out his hand to Jake.

"Benny Takada."

"Jake Kelman. Thanks for coming."

"My pleasure. It's great to meet you." Benny turned toward Quinn. Instead of a handshake, they drew each other in a quick bro hug. "How's it all going?"

"Nothing to complain about. Do you want a quick tour before we go inside?"

"That'd be great."

"I'll meet you two inside." Jake left the two alone, his booted feet eating up the space between them and the nearest corral.

"We'll start at the big barn." Quinn walked through the large enclosure, pointing out specialized stalls, storage for tack and various medications. "We aren't too far from town, but Jake's more comfortable keeping some medications in the small refrigerator."

"Smart. I've found most ranchers know a great deal about treating cattle and horses. Tell me about Jake."

"What do you want to know?" They walked into bright sunlight.

"How is he to work for? Does he have a solid background in the cattle business? Is he serious about adding Wagyu? Does he have the bandwidth to market the product? If you're the foreman, who's going to make pitches to restaurants and specialty grocers?" Benny shrugged. "Anything you believe would be helpful."

Quinn walked toward a corral where one of the men worked with a three-year-old colt. "He's a great boss. Grew up on a ranch, and worked the rodeo circuit for a few years before being hired at Whistle Rock Ranch. The Bonners are astute businesspeople, as well as ranchers. They can't say enough about him. He's helping with their horse breeding and cattle operations, and running their guest ranch business."

Benny's brows raised. "Dude ranch?"

"Yep. They're going into their second year, and reservations are already at almost eighty percent. They've had to turn some large groups away because of lack of cabin capacity. Right now, they're building additional cabins to handle increased demand."

"And you're running Kelman Ranch?"

"I am. Are you ready to go inside and talk details with Jake?"

A smile appeared on Benny's face. "I'm ready."

Aiden Winters laid out the images he'd taken over the last week. He'd identified most of the men working at Whistle Rock Ranch. Aiden always thought it amazing what sharing beers and conversation with other men could get you.

It had taken weeks of constant hunting to locate his prey. Now, he could take his time planning how to approach the Bonners. He'd yet to announce himself to the sheriff, a professional courtesy whenever he intended to recover a fugitive in a new jurisdiction. Aiden vowed to get that done soon.

Taking a seat at the small desk in the hotel room, Aiden opened the file. It had been a strange case from the start, pitting brother against brother. Making it even more intriguing was the fact they were twins.

His employer, the owner of the bail bond business, had assured him the capture would be quick and easy.

Aiden had learned the assessment wasn't accurate. The fugitive could be tough, and would fight to avoid being taken into custody.

"Bring it on," Aiden whispered as he continued through the file.

The odd part was how David Nielsen's twin brother had been convicted of the crime he'd committed. David hadn't come forward to confess, choosing to leave the state.

During a subsequent investigation, a witness had come forward to tell authorities they'd prosecuted the wrong twin. Blake wasn't the guilty party. That dishonor belonged to his brother, David.

Blake had been released, disappearing into the wind. David had been taken into custody, charged, and released on a bond with the assurance he'd appear on the scheduled court date. He hadn't shown.

Aiden had been sent after him soon after. Weeks had passed before a man at another ranch identified David, steering Aiden to Whistle Rock Ranch.

The identification came with a warning. "Don't assume the Bonners will turn him over without substantial, verified evidence."

Aiden was about to discover how loyal the Bonners could be.

Chapter Six

Abigail's brows drew together as she concentrated on crimping the edges of the second cherry pie planned for dinner. Two blackberry and a banana cream were cooling.

It was "pie night" at the ranch. A ranch hand favorite.

They were encouraged to provide suggestions for pies, and if available, recipes. Beth received at least four ideas each week.

Abigail loved pie night. Though she'd watched the owner of the diner in Sheridan bake, she'd never been allowed to prepare them herself. Beth let her make whatever desserts she chose, as long as they complemented the menu.

Baking kept her mind off struggles she didn't want to confront. Right now, the problem which took up too much of her thoughts was Quinn. He crept into her conscious off and on all day. Memories of them kept her awake at night, which created a huge issue for someone who had to rise early each morning.

She'd considered confronting him, shoving the idea aside each time. What would she say? It had been her, not Quinn, who'd shut down communication between them. She'd just have to deal with the regret over their breakup.

"Those pies look gorgeous, and the aroma is even better. Is that the last one?" Beth nodded toward the unbaked cherry pie.

Abigail nodded. "This is the last one. There are a few, maybe one or two, ranch hands who aren't pie eaters. I have carrot cake for them." She glanced to the counter next to one of the large refrigerators. "They're out of luck if they don't like carrot cake."

"Agreed. With lunch over, I decided to get a head start on dinner."

"I've defrosted the steaks and chicken."

"Excellent. I'm going to use a new rub for the steaks. I've decided to marinate the chicken using your orange juice and herbs recipe. It was a real hit last time. Do you have time to prepare red potatoes with garlic and rosemary?"

"Lots of time. You also mentioned asparagus. Do you want me to take care of it, also?"

"I'll prepare it if you'll assemble the salad."

"No problem, Beth."

The kitchen quieted as the women worked. Several minutes passed before Abigail raised her head, cocking it to one side. Listening a moment, she gave a slight shake of her head and continued the work in front of her.

Another minute passed before she raised her head again. "Did you hear that?"

"Hear what?" Beth asked.

"An odd whining sound. I think it's coming from outside."

"No. I didn't hear anything."

"Strange." Abigail walked to the sink, grabbing a bottle of water from the counter. Twisting off the top, she drank several swallows before recapping it. Standing there a little longer than necessary, she strained to hear the noise again.

Stepping back to where she'd been slicing tomatoes for the salad, she forgot about the odd sound. Placing the tomato slices in an airtight container, she removed lettuce and arugula from the refrigerator. She started to adjust the commercial vegetable slicer when she heard the whining noise again.

Beth looked at her. "I did hear that."

Both women stopped what they were doing to head to the back door. Opening it, Beth peered out.

"Oh my." Beth stepped outside. "What on earth?"

Abigail followed, stopping at the sight of a small box. Inside were three puppies. "They can't be more than five or six weeks old."

Glancing around, she dashed to the back of the building, then to the rear of nearby cabins, finding nothing. She took a slow turn around, trying to locate whoever put the box at the back door. Frustrated, Abigail returned to where Beth stood with the box in her hands.

"Did you see anybody?"

She shook her head at Beth. "Nothing. They had a lot of time to get away. It's been at least ten minutes since I heard the first sounds." Lowering her gaze to the tiny creatures, she stroked their fur with the backs of her fingers. "Do you think they could be weaned already?"

"Possibly. The thing is, I can't imagine someone dumping them on our doorstep if they still needed their mother."

"People do strange things, Beth. Should I call Doc Worrel? Maybe she'll have time to drive out."

"I hate bothering her. Let's try giving them milk first. If they're able to eat, then my guess is they're older than we think. If they can't take any food, then I'll ask Wyatt or Virgil if one of the ranch hands can take them to her clinic."

Beth made a liquid gruel of cooked rice cereal and water. Pouring the mixture into a small bowl, she set it on the floor before lifting each of the puppies out of the box. The bowl was licked clean several minutes later.

"They're eating, but I'd still like Doc Worrel to see them."

Abigail bent to pick up one of the puppies. "I'll take them between breakfast and lunch tomorrow." She snuggled her cheek into the puppy's fur. "So sweet."

"I know. What do you think they are?"

"What breed? Gosh, I don't know. Maybe a mix, but I'll leave that up to Doc Worrel." Setting the puppy back in the towel lined box, she looked around. "We could put them in the corner over there for now. I'll move them into my place when I go to bed. That way, I can check on them at night."

Abigail lived in an apartment behind the kitchen. Small and efficient, it suited her needs and was included as part of her employment.

"Do you think we should try to find who left them?"

Beth stared down at the three puppies. "I wouldn't know how to start. Assuming they're who left the box, I doubt they'd want the puppies back. Ask Dr. Worrel if she's heard of any puppies who are missing."

"Good idea."

"Well, we'd better get back to fixing dinner." Beth returned to the counter while Abigail placed the box in a corner of the kitchen.

Picking up where she left off with the vegetable chopper, she worked through the containers of items that would make up the evening's salad. When finished, she wrapped everything, placing the food in the refrigerator.

All she had left to prepare were the red potatoes with garlic and rosemary. Another dish the cowboys loved. She'd found it satisfying to prepare food for men who'd eat almost anything and be grateful for it. So unlike cooking in a restaurant, where customers would send food back to the kitchen for the slightest cause.

Beth didn't look up from assembling the asparagus in two large baking dishes. "After you finish the potatoes, go ahead and take some time off. Are you comfortable telling Virgil about what we found?"

"If you're talking about the puppies, no worries. I doubt he'll care. The question will be what we do with them."

It was a question which continued to roll across her mind throughout the day.

Quinn laid the last of the fifty-pound supplement bags on the existing stack, standing back to check the height. Satisfied, he lifted another bag from the back of his pickup.

"Pretty good, boss."

Quinn smiled at the oldest ranch hand. He and a few others had stayed after Jake purchased the ranch from Seth Magnus. On a beautiful, clear winter day a month earlier, the longtime Wyoming rancher had succumbed to the cancer which ravaged his body. Over two hundred people from miles around attended his services.

"Got to keep up with you, Grandy." Quinn set the last bag on the stack, wiping his hands down his jeans. "We have a load of alfalfa and Bermuda hay arriving after lunch. I'd like you to guide the driver to the covered yard. If there's too much hay for that area, have them unload it in the stack yard."

"Sure thing, boss." Giving a two-finger salute, the older man took off toward the barn.

Even with snow on the ground, Quinn swiped sweat from his brow. Moving bales of hay took a good deal of energy, and he was close to the end of his. Hearing an engine, he glanced toward the drive, seeing a white truck he didn't recognize. Parking in an open area, the door opened enough for him to see who was behind the wheel. A smile brightened his face.

"Hey, Sam." Pulling off his gloves, he met her as she stepped to the ground. "How are you?"

"Doing great." She looked around as she slid the keys into a pocket. "Some of the boys are heading to town for burgers. I was elected to invite you to come along."

He started to shake his head, then stopped. Quinn couldn't come up with a reason he shouldn't take off for a while. Friday night and his chores were finished.

"I have to clean up."

"No problem. They're all doing the same. We're going to Dulcy's. Do you know the place?"

"The grill in the middle of town. Right?"

"That's it. I can wait while you get ready, or we'll meet you there."

"I'll meet you there, Sam."

"Sounds good." Climbing back into the truck, she leaned out the window. "See you in about thirty minutes."

"You got it." Watching as she turned the truck around, Quinn headed inside.

He couldn't recall the last time he'd been out with other ranch hands. All were good people, and he especially liked Sam. Unpretentious and a hard worker, she always wore a smile. According to Jake, she fit in with the other ranch hands real well. If she didn't already have a job at Whistle Rock, Quinn would swoop her up for Kelman Ranch.

Showered and dressed twenty minutes later, he hopped into his truck after leaving a note for Jake and Beth. Passing the driveway to Whistle Rock Ranch, he spotted Abigail's car, and wondered about her plans for the weekend.

He knew she'd had at least two dates with Doctor Mason Nagle. The thought soured his mood before he shook it off. Abigail was free to spend time with whoever she chose. Quinn had hoped she might have sought him out, interested in talking about what happened between them. She hadn't.

Parking in Dulcy's lot, he climbed out at the same time Sam pulled in next to him. She exited the cab, the familiar smile flashing at him.

"Hey, Quinn. Perfect timing." She walked to the entrance with him keeping pace beside her. "The others should already be here." Inside, she scanned the large dining room. "There they are. Looks like they saved chairs for us."

Quinn followed Sam's gaze. The smile froze on his face.

Abigail sat at the table, an empty chair beside her.

Chapter Seven

Abigail laughed at something Blake Nielsen said, picked up her glass of water, and glanced around the room. Her hand froze partway to her mouth. Quinn stared straight at her.

Inactive butterflies in her stomach roared to life at the intensity in his emerald green eyes. It took her a moment to shake off the affect he had on her. Setting the glass down, she worked to hide her unease. It seemed to be working until he took the empty chair next to her.

"I assume this is an open seat."

Swallowing the uncomfortable lump in her throat, she nodded.

He tilted his head to get a better view of her. "Yes, it's open?"

"Um, yes." Her attempt to scoot her chair away from him failed. Quinn was just too big not to suck up all the space between Abigail and the ranch hand on the other side of him.

"How are you, Abbie?"

"Good. I'm...good." She winced at the way her voice faltered. "Busy. I was surprised Beth gave me the evening off. I guess with half the ranch hands eating out tonight, she decided I wasn't needed." Grabbing her water glass, she gulped until it was empty.

Without asking, Quinn picked up the pitcher, filling her glass and topping off his own.

"Thank you." Taking a short sip, she set down her glass.

"I was surprised to see you here. Thought you'd still be working or out with Doc Nagle."

"Beth gave me the night off. I wasn't planning to go anywhere until Blake mentioned a group of them coming here."

The waitress set a glass filled with beer in front of Quinn. "Thanks, ma'am."

The tall, slender, middle-aged woman tucked a strand of graying brown hair behind her ear and smiled. "Either of you two ready to order dinner?"

"Do you know what you want, Abbie?"

Ignoring Quinn, she spoke to the waitress. "Cheeseburger with lettuce and tomato. And sweet potato fries. And I'd like my own check, please."

"No problem." The waitress looked at Quinn. "And you?"

"The same, but with regular fries."

"I'll get those right out to you."

"I could've paid for your food, Abbie."

She stared at him as if he had a second head. "That isn't going to happen. I pay my own way."

"Fine by me." Sipping his beer, he focused on the conversation about an upcoming rodeo.

Several minutes passed as they waited for their food while speaking with others around the table. When the various conversations slowed, Abigail bit her bottom lip as if making a decision.

"How do you like working for Jake?"

"He's a great guy. The truth is, I don't see him much. He leaves most decisions up to me."

She gave a slow nod. "Beth said you're going to add Wagyu beef."

"That was my recommendation to Jake. He's still considering the numbers Benny gave him."

Both quieted when the waitress set down their plates. Thanking her, they busied themselves adding condiments to their burgers. Quinn's first bite brought a smile to his face.

"These are the best burgers this side of Denver," he said before taking another large bite.

Abigail almost choked on her drink. "You used to say that about the burgers at the diner."

"Well, they're as good as these." Reaching for one of the paper napkins, he wiped mustard from the corners of his mouth. Seeing the skeptical expression on her face, he tried again. "The burgers at the diner were great. Probably still great. These," he held out what was left of his food, "are amazing. He must use the smoker at the beginning or end of cooking them."

Taking another bite, she tested his theory. "I think you're right." Smiling, she popped a sweet potato fry in her mouth.

Quinn watched her, his chest squeezing. There'd been a time when all their conversations were full of laughter. Her smile would light up a room...and his heart.

From the end of the table, Virgil stood. "Hey, everyone! A big storm is coming through. Best finish up and get back to the ranch."

"Oh no." Abigail set down the last of her burger. "My ride won't be here for another hour."

"I'll take you."

She shook her head. "No. I'll find something."

"No need to ask around. I have my truck, and I'm driving right by Whistle Rock."

"Well..."

"We'll finish our meals and leave. It's an easy solution, Abbie."

He was right about it being a no-brainer. The problem was they'd be alone for at least fifteen minutes in a tight space. The thought had her heart racing, fear coursing through her.

"Nothing's going to happen except you getting a ride to the ranch."

She didn't feel like arguing over something so insignificant. "All right. Are you ready?"

He nodded. "If you are." Standing, he reached for her chair.

"I can do it." The legs scraped on the wood floor as she pushed back and stood. Lifting her purse from where it hung on the back of the chair, she walked past him to the entrance.

Quinn opened the door and whistled. "Virgil wasn't exaggerating when he said a storm was coming. I'll pull the truck up here."

"No need. I can make it." Taking off to her right, she stopped at his yell.

"It's five down on the left, Abbie."

Whirling around, she rushed to his truck, hearing the door unlock. She climbed inside, but not without carrying in a good amount of snow with her.

Quinn closed her door before hurrying around to his side. He brought slightly less snow than her into the truck before slamming his door closed. Starting the engine, he didn't rush out of the parking lot.

"This is a mid-winter blizzard." Abigail leaned forward, unable to see more than ten feet in front of them. "It's getting worse."

"I know."

Glancing at him, she hid a smile before returning her attention to the storm. "I don't think we're going to make it to the ranch."

"Sure we will." His words sounded more confident than he felt. The odds were good they'd have to pull off the road, waiting until the storm passed.

Gripping the steering wheel, he leaned forward, losing the road for several seconds in the blinding snow. Spotting the large, neon sign for a motel on the right, he made a quick decision. He made a slow turn into the lot, glad for all the lights around the property.

"The storm is picking up, Abbie. We'll stay here until it passes."

"At a motel?"

"That's what this is."

"I don't know, Quinn. It doesn't sound right."

"We'll get one room with two beds. I'll stay awake for as long as I can. When the storm breaks, I'll wake you up and we'll leave."

"Two beds?"

"Yes."

"I guess there isn't much of a choice, is there?"

"We can stay in the car..." He let the idea trail off, seeing her mouth twist in disgust.

"This is a real nice truck. But it will get cramped and cold."

"Right. So, we're good for getting a room?"

Letting out a long sigh, she nodded.

"Everyone is back except for Quinn and Abbie." Jake's voice held an edge of concern.

Beth touched her husband's arm. "She rode out with one of the ranch hands whose girlfriend lives in town. She planned to ride back with someone from the ranch. If it is Quinn, he'll make sure your sister is safe."

"There are all kinds of safety, Beth." Pacing to the window, he shook his head in disgust. "The storm isn't letting up."

"My guess is he is waiting it out. I'll try calling him."

Jake pulled his phone from a pocket. "And I'll call Abbie."

"I can't get through, Jake. The storm must be messing with the signal."

"Same here. I can't even leave a message. I'll try again in a few minutes. Do we have any coffee?"

"I'll fix you a cup." Beth headed to the kitchen, her stomach churning at not being able to speak with either Abigail or Quinn.

When stressed, Beth's solution had always been to busy herself in the kitchen. Cakes, pies, cookies. Anything which didn't require a trip to the grocery store.

Waiting for the coffee to finish brewing, she absently checked ingredients in the cupboards. She could make almost anything with what was already stocked. Not that she'd reached that level of stress. Beth felt certain they'd get through to Abigail and Quinn before too long.

Instead of the storm clearing, it increased to blizzard level. No calls in or out.

"I can drive to Whistle Rock and borrow one of their SAT phones." Jake stood at a window.

"Does it matter if Quinn doesn't have one?" Handing him the cup filled with hot coffee, she sat down in an overstuffed chair facing the front windows.

"No. SAT phones can call any phone number."

"It's brutal out there, Jake. Maybe wait a little longer to see if the storm passes us. My guess is Quinn found a place to stay until they can drive back."

"That's assuming they're together." Scrubbing both hands down his face, Jake continued to pace.

Beth agreed. "If it will make you feel better, we'll both drive to Whistle Rock and use a SAT phone."

"I'd appreciate it."

Grabbing her coat, she headed to the front door. "Let's get going. The sooner we talk to one of them, the sooner we'll be able to relax."

Abigail sat on a chair she'd moved to the front window, hands clasped in her lap, attention focused outside. Instead of easing, the storm had picked up to the point where she couldn't make out anything in the parking lot.

"I can't recall a blizzard this strong."

He moved to stand beside her, his features blank as he surveyed the intensity of the storm. "Neither can I, Abbie. We're lucky they had a room left."

She breathed out a snort. "I suppose it was luck we got the last one." Glancing up at him, then to the bed, she offered a small smile. "With two beds."

Dropping down beside the chair, he met her curious stare. "This would be a good time to talk about what happened between us."

Jumping up, she walked as far away from Quinn as the small room would allow. He followed, staying a few feet away.

"I want to understand why you never responded to any of my messages, Abbie. Please. Talk to me."

Chapter Eight

Lowering herself onto one of the beds, Abigail wrapped both arms around her waist. She couldn't meet his expectant gaze.

"Abbie?"

She heard the question in Quinn's voice, but didn't respond. Except for blinking eyelids, she sat as still as a stone.

Discussing the past made her shiver with cold. She'd messed everything up by not responding to any of his messages. If anger at his leaving hadn't controlled her actions, they might still be together. Trying to overcome the past seemed an insurmountable obstacle. One Abigail wasn't sure she wanted to tackle.

Wouldn't it be better for them to move on and forget their short history? She risked a glance at Quinn. He hadn't shifted his gaze from her face. Whatever stopped her from confronting the fear, which often ruled her actions, hadn't subsided when Quinn's phone rang.

A look of frustration crossed his face an instant before he answered. "Yeah?"

"Quinn, it's Jake."

He stood, moving to the window. "What's going on?"

"Where are you, and is Abbie with you?"

Quinn heard the worry in his boss's voice, and winced. "We're together. I should've called."

"Where are you?"

"Mountain Rest Motel. I couldn't see a foot ahead of us, so we decided to wait the storm out." Looking outside, Quinn realized the blizzard had quieted to a moderate snowstorm. "We'll be on our way to the ranch in a few minutes. Do you want to speak to Abbie?"

"I'll wait until you drop her off at the ranch. I'm borrowing a SAT phone from the Bonners, so Beth and I will stay put until you get here."

"Sounds good. We'll be there soon." Ending the call, his attention switched to Abigail. He sighed, knowing the conversation he so wanted to happen would have to be put off. Again.

Abigail took in Beth's words about the puppies, ignoring the tears burning at the back of her eyes. Glancing outside, she concentrated on the beautiful spring morning instead of the disappointment she felt at the news.

"I'm sorry, Abbie. I didn't know what else to do." Beth's features showed the guilt at what had transpired. "Doc Worrel called to tell us the puppies had been claimed by a local breeder. She knows him. Apparently, they'd been stolen by an ex-employee."

Abigail stopped kneading pie dough to lean against the counter. "Why come all the way out here to leave them?"

"The breeder didn't know. Doc Worrel believes the person who stole them thought the Bonners would take good care of them. They were right, of course. Still, it doesn't make sense to me."

Abigail didn't respond. She'd planned to adopt one of the puppies, already had a name picked out and purchased a collar. It wasn't meant to be. She felt silly having such a strong reaction to losing the opportunity to own one of the puppies.

"There's a Humane Society located in Jackson. We should drive over there so you can pick out a dog."

Tipping her head back, Abigail stared at the ceiling. "I don't really need a dog, Beth. The puppies were cute and needed someone to care for them. I'm glad the owner was found."

"If you change your mind, we'll plan a trip to Jackson."

Continuing to knead the dough, Abigail's lips drew into a tight smile. "Thank you, but it's fine, Beth. A dog would be an added responsibility I don't need right now."

Deciding to let it go, Beth returned to her own work. "I've never offered a hearty salad, bread, soup, and dessert for lunch. I sure hope the ranch hands like it."

"The salad is heavy with chunks of beef, pork, and chicken. Paired with soup and artisan bread, and I'm sure everyone will be satisfied, Beth."

Talk of food reminded Abigail of a few nights earlier, when she'd sat next to Quinn at the restaurant. The first minutes were uncomfortable, then she'd forced herself to relax. Being near him hadn't been as difficult as anticipated. Neither had their time together in the motel as they waited for the storm to pass.

Their return to the ranch had been anticlimactic. He'd opened her door, helped her out, then gone to speak with Jake and Beth. She'd been left with nothing to do except return to her apartment behind the kitchen.

The letdown had been a surprise. She'd felt adrift, and very much alone. Until that night, she'd been too exhausted to feel lonely.

Jake's call had saved her from explaining the immature reactions to Quinn's messages from Idaho. Abigail didn't understand why she'd never responded to his calls, emails, and texts. He'd been important to her, knew about his goal of finding a job that would utilize his education.

Changing into sleeping pants and a tank top, she stretched out under the covers. For the first time in days, she thought of Mason Nagle. They were going out for dinner on Friday to a steakhouse between Brilliance and Jackson. It was supposed to be beautiful inside, and the menu unlike any in the region.

Abigail couldn't marshal even a small amount of enthusiasm for their date. Not that she didn't like Mason, because she did. The problem was the reappearance of Quinn.

She'd been in love with him when he left for Idaho. It took the evening at the restaurant to realize her love had never died.

Did he feel the same? Abigail didn't know. Did the fact he wanted answers point to a continued interest in her? Maybe.

Quinn didn't ask to see her again when they returned the night of the storm. Instead, he'd rushed toward Jake and Beth, letting Abigail return to her apartment alone. Not a big deal, but a sign he might not still hold deep feelings for her.

She reminded herself his curiosity didn't equate to love.

Passing Whistle Rock Ranch, Quinn bumped along the road to Jake and Beth's ranch. Snow from the storm had already melted, leaving the road a muddy mess. It wouldn't be long before the wildflowers appeared, giving the region a fresh look.

He'd loaded bags of grain and supplements into the back of his truck, not willing to wait for the feed and tack store to deliver. As he drove, he kept sending glances toward the Bonners' main lodge, disappointed when he didn't get a glimpse of Abigail.

They hadn't spoken for several days, since the evening of the storm. That was on him. Quinn had been hesitant to push her. Did it really matter why she ignored his messages when in Idaho? Those days were past. His time would be better spent concentrating on the future, figuring out if he and Abigail still had one.

Parking in a space near the feed shed, he jumped out and stopped. A truck came into view on the road from the Bonner ranch. Steel gray with an absence of chrome, it almost blended into the background. Quinn knew he'd never seen it before.

Coming to a stop a few feet from his truck, the driver got out, stretched, and walked around the front to face Quinn. He held out his hand.

"I'm Aiden Winters."

"Quinn Sawyer. What can I do for you?"

Aiden withdrew a folded piece of paper, handing it to Quinn. "I'm looking for that man, and believe he's working at Whistle Rock Ranch. Do you recognize him?"

Opening the wanted poster, he stared at the photograph of a handsome, yet stern man. He had seen someone who resembled the image, but was hesitant to get in the middle of whatever the bounty hunter was cooking up.

"I've never worked at the Bonner place. You'd do better to show it to Wyatt Bonner or Virgil Redstar. They're the ones who hire the ranch hands." Handing back the wanted poster, he reached into the back of the truck for a sack of grain.

"Wyatt Bonner. He's one of the owners?"

"Yeah."

"Who's Virgil Redstar?"

"The foreman. Look, I have a lot of work to do. It would be best if you talked to them."

Touching the brim of his cowboy hat, Aiden smiled. "Appreciate the information."

Quinn didn't respond as he took the sack into the feed shed. Returning, he watched as the truck disappeared down the road. Tugging out his phone, he called Jake.

"A bounty hunter named Aiden Winters was just here. He had a wanted poster for Blake Nielsen. I believe he's headed to Whistle Rock." After an appreciative response from Jake, he ended the call.

It wasn't that Quinn didn't approve of bounty hunters. On the surface, they were doing what law enforcement didn't have time or the manpower to handle. Budgets were tight, and fewer people were applying for what could be a dangerous and undervalued job. Bounty hunters filled the gap.

Still, there were some who went about their business on the edge of legal boundaries. He didn't know if Winters was one of those, but a heads-up to Jake wouldn't hurt.

Reaching once more into the back of the truck, he continued to move feed into the shed, letting Aiden Winters, and his business, vanish from his thoughts.

Virgil, Wyatt, Jake, and Blake Nielsen sat in Wyatt's office, the wanted poster spread out on the desk. Aiden

Winters had been turned away after introducing himself to Wyatt. He and Virgil knew it was a reprieve, not a surrender.

Resting his arms on the desk, Virgil leaned toward Blake. "Is that you?"

Heart pounding, sweat forming on his brow, Blake stared at the photograph. "Yes, but it's an old poster."

"What does that mean?" Wyatt tapped a finger on the desk.

His breathing turned erratic as he searched for what to say. Blake's granddaddy had always told him to start with the truth and go from there.

"My twin brother, David, is who you're looking at on the poster. Unfortunately, they arrested me. I went to prison, then got out when the authorities realized they had the wrong man. It never should've gone as far as it did."

"No one came forth to prove they had the wrong man?" Jake asked.

"Plenty of people told them they had it all wrong. My granddaddy even spoke to the district attorney directly. The woman waved him off as old and demented. Everyone had made up their minds."

Wyatt pulled the paper closer, scanning it one more time. "What happened?"

"Granddaddy never gave up. He spent most of his money to hire a new defense attorney. An impressive man you couldn't ignore. They produced enough strong evidence that the district attorney couldn't look the other way any longer. My guess is they're now looking for David. The bounty hunter is chasing the wrong Nielsen brother."

"Do you have anything with you that proves what you've said?"

"In my cabin, Virgil. A scrapbook of the entire misadventure, including an article about charges being dropped and my release."

"Jake, go with Blake to retrieve the scrapbook." Wyatt looked at Blake. "I'm trusting you're telling us the truth, so don't try running. Get the evidence and bring it back here. I want everything needed to get this Winters fella back on the road toward the right brother."

Chapter Nine

"Hey, Quinn." He turned to see Sam Miller emerge from the barn, a bridle in one hand.

"How are you, Sam?"

"Great. Love working here. The people are great. How are you doing?"

"Same." He risked a glance at the kitchen's back door. "We may be adding to our stock soon."

"I heard about it from Jake. It seems a good idea to me to diversify when most of your sales are to restaurants and grocers in the western U.S. Will you be expanding the marketing area?"

Quinn threw back his head on a hearty laugh. "Let's cross one hurdle at a time, Sam. First, we have to buy the cattle."

She joined him in laughing. "You're right. I have a tendency to jump ahead. Actually, I wanted to let you know about a softball league that starts up in the spring. The Bonners always sponsor a team from the ranch. Uniforms, equipment...the usual. I heard you used to play in high school. We'd love to have you on the team."

"Wow. I haven't thrown a ball in years."

"About half our team hasn't played for years, so you'd fit right in."

Excitement at the prospect of playing again coursed through him. "My job comes first, Sam. If there's a conflict, I'm going to choose the ranch over the game."

"No different from the rest of us. What position did you play in high school?"

"Pitcher, but that was fastball, not softball. I've also played short stop and second base."

"Great. We only have one of the ranch hands who's pitched before, and he'd rather play in the field. Are you still interested in pitching?"

Quinn's mouth twisted as he thought about pitching in a softball league. He couldn't think of a single reason why he shouldn't sign up. "I'll need a little practice."

Her face lit up on a broad smile. "Is that a yes?"

"Yeah. It's a yes."

"Yahoo!" she shouted, garnering attention from a group of ranch hands mending the corral fence. "I'll put you down. Our first practice is Friday night at seven at the city field. Do you know where that is?"

"Nope, but I can figure it out."

"No need. You can ride with me. Just be here at five-thirty. I'd better get back to my work, Quinn. Glad you're going to join us."

"Same here. See you Friday." He took off toward the barn to speak with Jake about a possible delivery for their new program. The corners of his mouth tilted upward at the thought of throwing a ball again. Friday couldn't come soon enough.

Abigail stood back from the kitchen window, wondering what Quinn and Sam had been talking about. Whatever they discussed, it brought a grin to Quinn's face and an added bounce to his step as he walked toward the group of men exiting the barn.

She peeked out once more, seeing him meet up with Jake. The two headed off by themselves, prompting her to return to marinating chicken for the dinner menu.

A few minutes passed before a knock on the kitchen door preceded Sam stepping inside. She told Abigail about the softball team.

"I don't know, Sam. It's been a long time since I played softball."

"It's the same with most of us, Abbie. What position did you play?"

"Catcher."

"Wow. That would be great. We don't have anyone else who's played that position. The first practice is this Friday at seven at the community fields."

"I can't this Friday, but let me know when the next practice is and I'll consider joining."

"It will be the following Friday. We may add another day. I'll let you know. Thanks, Abbie. Hope you can join us."

She watched Sam leave, feeling a trickle of excitement.

"Did Sam talk to you about the softball team?" Beth set a bag of onions on the counter next to the commercial slicing machine.

"She did. Are you going to join?"

Beth laughed. "Me? I tried it in grade school and couldn't throw a ball at a target. Well, I could throw it, but I couldn't hit the target." She chuckled again. "I'd miss by a big margin. No, I'll be happy sitting in the stands, watching you play."

"What about Jake?"

"He's going to the practice on Friday. I may watch that, too. We're going to barbecue and use paper plates and utensils, so cleanup will be fast. Do you still have your date with Mason?"

"As far as I know."

"I'm sure you'll have a great time." Beth turned away to prepare the onions for the slicer.

Abigail finished with the chicken before preparing the vegetable dish Beth had decided on. She tried to concentrate on her work, though her thoughts kept returning to Quinn.

The way her thoughts kept being hijacked to him irritated her. Abigail didn't want to think about Quinn. They weren't a couple, and barely spoke to each other.

What bothered her most was she wanted him to ask her out. He hadn't. Not even come close to showing an interest in spending time with her. Quinn wanted answers to her not returning his messages. He didn't want to spend dinner or any other time with her. She needed to accept this and move on.

Which meant being excited about her date with Mason. She truly did enjoy the doctor's company. Bright, handsome, with an excellent sense of humor, he was a man any single woman would be proud to be seen with. It didn't hurt he was a doctor with an excellent reputation.

Abigail prepared the vegetables in two restaurant-sized pans, forcing thoughts of Quinn from her mind. She'd experience the steakhouse with Mason, enjoy the food, and the company.

Friday appeared as a beautiful day, with clear skies and warm air. The muddy ruts from the recent storm had begun to dry out. If the weather stayed clear, they'd order the road from the highway be scraped, packed, and oiled. It was a ritual performed every spring after the last of the storms.

Quinn ate an early breakfast of eggs, ham, potatoes, toast, and coffee, leaving the house before Jake and Beth made their way to the kitchen. He'd told them about his intention to participate with Bonner ranch hands on the softball team. Jake mentioned they'd be there to watch the games.

Tonight was their first practice. Quinn couldn't deny he felt a surge of anticipation at the prospect of throwing a ball again. He loved the work at Kelman Ranch. With little interest in dating anyone except Abigail, he welcomed the distraction of playing softball.

Finishing his chores at six, he showered before driving the short distance to Whistle Rock Ranch. Sam waited by her truck with another ranch hand. Blake Nielsen.

The sight of the man on the wanted poster surprised Quinn. He'd learned from Jake the ranch hand had produced a binder with a complete history of what had transpired from his arrest to his release. The documentation also included details on the differences between Blake and his twin brother, David.

"Quinn, this is Blake Nielsen. Blake, Quinn Sawyer. Both of you have experience pitching in high school, which is great. We'll always have a backup. Climb in and I'll get us to the community park."

Again, Quinn thought of how much he liked Sam, especially her enthusiasm for anything. If he wasn't so hung-up on Abigail, he'd be tempted to ask her out.

"When was the last time you threw a ball, Quinn?" Blake had taken the passenger seat across from Sam.

"Not since high school. This is going to be a real challenge. What about you?"

"I played a little at the community college, and a short time at another place where I lived. But it's been a while."

Quinn recalled a picture in the scrapbook of Blake playing in his prison garb. "How do you like working at Whistle Rock?"

"It's great. Best place I've ever worked." Blake fell silent.

Quinn could only imagine what the man was thinking about. Falsely accused of a crime he didn't commit, convicted, and sent to prison. Although the stay wasn't long, it would've been tough.

"Do you have a family?" Quinn asked.

"Me? Nah. I'm as single as they come. Maybe someday..." His voice trailed off, and again, Quinn thought of how difficult the last few years had been for Blake. "What about you?"

"Never married. If this job at Jake's ranch works out, maybe I'll start looking around."

"You two don't have to look far." Sam's voice held a trace of mischief. "Abigail's single and a real beauty. If we're lucky, she may decide to join the team. She was the catcher for her high school team. I think she played some community ball in Sheridan."

Quinn knew she did from the time they were a couple. She'd wanted him to join the team. He never had the time. Maybe he could make up for his mistake by pitching for the ranch team.

"What do you think of Abigail, Quinn?"

He spotted Sam glancing at him in the rearview mirror, and shrugged. "She seems like a great gal. I know she can cook."

Blake shifted in his seat to look at Quinn. "She sure can. Best pies I've ever tasted. The problem is, she's way out of my league. And she makes this Mexican casserole that's crazy good. She's learned to make double the amount, as everyone goes back for seconds."

Quinn knew which casserole Blake meant. She used to fix it for him on her days off at the diner. So darn many memories.

"Here we are." Sam pulled into a large parking area, already more than halfway filled with vehicles. "Looks like we aren't the only ones who decided to practice tonight."

"This is great." Blake opened his door. "We'll be able to get a sense of our competition."

"The equipment should be at the A2 dugout." Sam nodded to their right, where several people from the ranch stood around, talking.

The three wasted no time crossing the lot to join the others. Sam appeared to be the organizer, though she declined when nominated as the group's coach.

"Virgil, you should step up and be the manager." Barrel clasped him on the back. "You're used to ordering us around." Laughter followed, though it was obvious the others agreed with Barrel.

A broad grin appeared on Virgil's face. "Wyatt isn't here yet. We should elect him."

Barrel nodded with enthusiasm. "Great idea! All in favor of Wyatt being the manager, say aye."

Everyone agreed.

"Those who disagree, say nay."

The group fell silent.

Virgil laughed. "It's agreed, then. Wyatt is the manager, as well as an outfielder."

Owen cleared his throat. "Has he ever played, Virgil?"

"Not that I recall. But neither have I."

Another round of laughter followed his confession. They quieted when one of the ranch hands elbowed the man beside him. Within seconds, all the men were staring past Quinn.

"She sure does clean up well," one said over a crooked grin.

"Who knew? She's always wearing an apron with her hair up," another of the men added.

The last comment had Quinn doing a slow turn, his breath catching when he saw who approached. Abigail approached in tight jeans and a form fitting blouse, which snapped up the front. Black boots encased her feet, a pair of tennis shoes in one hand. Her steps faltered only a bit when she spotted Quinn.

"Hope I'm not late."

"Abbie," Barrel said. "You're right on time."

Chapter Ten

Abigail's heart thumped at the intense gaze from Quinn. It reminded her of how he'd always made her believe she was the most beautiful woman wherever they went.

Sam made room for Abbie to stand next to her. "I heard you couldn't make it. A date or something?"

"You heard right. The date was cancelled."

"The guy must be an idiot to do that to you." Barrel shook his head in wonder.

"Oh, he's no idiot." She thought of Mason's last minute phone call, the regret in his voice at having to back out of their date. "Are we going to practice or just stand here?"

Virgil nodded in agreement. "You heard the lady. Grab your gear and let's get out on the field."

Abigail checked the writing on each of the bags, heading to the one marked catcher. Unlike some of the duffels, her position required enough gear to fill the entire space. Chest protector, helmet, leg guards, and catcher's mitt. It was all there, a reminder of her time in high school. She hadn't thought of those days in, well...years.

Virgil grabbed his mitt and faced the others. "How about we start with batting practice? Quinn will pitch, Abbie catch. The rest of us will split into batters and outfielders. Then we'll switch up."

"Works for me. I'll start in the infield." Sam slid her left hand into her glove, opening and closing it several times as she ran toward second base.

Abigail felt a hand on her shoulder and turned to face Quinn. "How about we get some practice in before the batters come up?"

Tightening her chest protector, she grabbed her helmet. "I could use about an hour of practice, but will settle for whatever I can get."

"Virgil, we're going to pitch and catch before the first batter comes up."

"Good idea, Quinn. Take as much time as you need."

The first batter stepped up to the plate ten minutes later. Owen gripped the bat as if he'd played his entire life. Pitch one went wide, much too far outside for Abigail to catch. The second was better, and Owen swung and missed. The third went right over the center of the plate. Owen swung, sending the ball past Sam at second base, and into centerfield.

Owen didn't run the bases. After watching the ball roll several yards, he took his position at home plate. This time, the ball flew into right field.

As it turned out, Owen was their best hitter. When they were finished, everyone had practiced their position in the field and taken at least twenty pitches. Tired and exhilarated, they piled into their vehicles, driving to the local pizza spot.

Abigail drove alone, giving herself time to think about baseball, Quinn, and Mason. The doctor had been apologetic and somewhat regretful, though he didn't sound as sorry as his words implied. Not that it mattered. Regardless of the pep talk she'd given herself, Abigail hadn't been as enthusiastic about their date as she'd hoped. His lack of asking for an alternate evening indicated he might feel the same.

Her feelings about Quinn were equally confusing. He'd had several opportunities to ask her out. The man she knew wouldn't have worried about rejection. He would've charged ahead, kept asking until she finally relented.

Abigail had to accept he no longer held an interest in her other than as a friend. He'd been great at baseball practice. Encouraging and friendly, providing bits of advice, which did prove helpful.

Opening the door to the pizza shack, she stalled at the raucous laughter. Several of the teams must've decided this was the best place to end their evening.

Glancing around, she spotted Quinn at a table across the room. Making her way through the throng of people, she stopped abruptly at the sight of a couple at a table in the corner.

Doctor Mason Nagle was in an animated discussion with a woman Abigail didn't recognize. She told herself it must be someone from the hospital. They finished their shifts and came here for a beer and pizza.

Stepping closer, she heard the woman exclaim how much she loved the movie they'd seen earlier. The truth hit her in the gut. Mason had cancelled their date not because of an additional shift at the hospital. He'd tossed her aside for a movie and dinner with another woman.

As the truth became clear, she began to turn away when Mason's voice sounded over the noise of the diners. He was by her side a moment later.

"Abbie, wait."

She didn't. Why hear Mason explain what she'd already figured out?

"Please, Abbie."

Letting out a deep breath, she turned to face him. "It's fine, Mason. You preferred spending the evening with someone else. It happens."

"Hey, Abbie! You're going to miss the pizza."

She looked over her shoulder to see Barrel motioning for her to join them. "I'd better get over there or I won't get any dinner."

Mason didn't try to stop her as she whirled around to leave him standing in the middle of the room. "I'll call you, Abbie."

Ignoring him, she smiled at Barrel and the others before taking a beer from Quinn's outstretched hand.

"Thanks."

Quinn swept a hand toward the seat next to him. "Sit down and eat before it's all gone."

She didn't argue. The first slice disappeared within a few minutes. The second took a little longer.

"This pizza is great."

"Sam comes here at least once a week. She placed the order tonight. That gal really knows her way around

Brilliance. She's also one of the best wranglers I've ever seen. I'm hoping to talk her into moving over to Jake's ranch at some point."

Abigail listened to Quinn list Sam's virtues as the pizza congealed in her stomach. She'd heard Wyatt and Virgil say much the same about their employee.

"Nothing rattles her, either."

Gritting her teeth, Abigail swallowed the last of her beer. Tempted to slam the glass on the wood table, she stopped herself and stood.

"That was great, but I'm out of here."

"Already?"

"I still have to get up early to fix breakfast for all these reprobates." She smiled as she said it. "Beth isn't coming in until about ten, so I'm on my own."

Quinn shoved his chair back and stood. "I'll walk you out."

She waved a hand. "Not needed. Enjoy your night."

Ignoring her attempt at putting him off, Quinn walked outside with her. "Something wrong, Abbie?"

"Nope. It was a good practice, followed by some great food. Thanks for all your suggestions. Feel free to keep them coming at the next practice." Reaching her vehicle, she climbed inside. "See you around, Quinn."

Watching her drive off, he wondered what had set her off. Despite what she said, he knew something troubled her, changing her mood. Blowing out a frustrated breath, he shook his head before returning to the restaurant.

85

Abigail's hands tightened on the steering wheel as she returned to Whistle Rock Ranch. The high degree of frustration bewildered her.

Practice was great. She looked forward to their next one, and the games to follow. Finding Mason on a date with another woman had been a letdown, though nothing close to shattering her spirit. Both of them were free to go out with anyone they wanted. She just wished he hadn't lied about it.

Quinn going on about Sam shouldn't have bothered her. She liked Sam, believed the female ranch hand was a great addition to Whistle Rock.

Her only excuse at the irritation was dismay at Mason's actions. Ridiculous and weak, yet it was all she could pin the frustration on. Except, that wasn't quite true.

The last few weeks had been a challenge, and in many ways disappointing.

At Beth's insistence, Abigail had applied to two culinary programs in Wyoming. Neither accepted her, though each encouraged she try again the following year. She'd been disappointed and a little relieved. Leaving the ranch for school would've been difficult, though Beth had assured her they could find someone to take over her work.

The puppies had been left at the kitchen door the following day, softening the setback of not being accepted into a culinary program. It hadn't taken long for her to select the perfect puppy for herself. Picking out a name and buying a collar had been easy, doubting they would be claimed. She'd been wrong.

As her mother had always done when life got tough, Abigail had put on her big girl pants and gotten back to work. Then Mason had lied about cancelling their date. In truth, she was more saddened by him not being truthful than taking out another woman.

Parking in her usual spot, Abigail didn't release the seatbelt right away. She'd been depressed for a long time after Quinn left for Idaho, and refused to go down that road again.

Ticking off the good things going on in her life, she found the list far outnumbered the setbacks. And neither list included Quinn.

Chapter Eleven

Abigail stopped dressing at the sound of loud voices outside her apartment. They weren't coming from the kitchen, where Beth would already be prepping for breakfast. She recognized at least one voice.

Most would classify Wyatt as slow to burn. It took a great deal for his color to rise, along with his words. That mystical line had been crossed this morning.

She grabbed a clean apron after leaving her apartment, tying it on while joining Beth. "What's going on outside?"

"I don't know all of it. You heard about a bounty hunter tracking down Blake, right?"

"A little bit. Virgil gave me an overview in case the bounty hunter showed up. Blake says the man is searching for his twin brother, David."

"Blake's story is he was misidentified as David. No matter the evidence provided by family and his doctor, he was convicted of a crime and sent to jail. He didn't spend much time there before his true identity was verified, and a warrant was issued for David."

Abigail pulled out a large skillet, adding a small amount of oil. "Apparently, the bounty hunter got steered to the wrong brother."

"That would be my guess." Sliding a carton of eighteen eggs out of the refrigerator, Beth placed them next to the frying pan. "He arrived early this morning and tried to rustle Blake out of the bunkhouse so he could cuff him. It didn't go over well. Wyatt, Virgil, and Jake are trying to set him straight using Blake's scrapbook."

"Scrapbook?"

"He documented the entire screwup on his computer, then placed hard copies into a scrapbook." Grabbing two loaves of bread, she placed eight pieces in a toaster.

Both women turned around when the back door opened. Jake, Wyatt, Virgil, and Blake were followed by a tall man with dark hair and a slight scar running from the outside edge of his left eye to the corner of his mouth. Wearing all black from his boots to his hat, he was the cliché of how a bounty hunter should look.

"Beth, would you mind getting coffee for all of us?" Jake placed a hand on the small of his wife's back. "We'll be in Wyatt's office."

"I'll get everything right to you."

"Thanks, sweetheart." Jake brushed his lips across her cheek before catching up with the others.

Beth stared after him. "Guess they're getting right down to sorting this out."

Abigail cracked eggs into a large bowl. "It's got to be hard on Blake. He served time for his brother's actions and is still being haunted by what happened."

"Changing the subject, tell me what went on Friday night with you and Quinn."

Shrugging, she finished cracking one pack of eggs before pulling another out of the refrigerator. "Not much to tell. We all met for softball practice. Quinn's a pitcher and I'm the catcher. Afterward, most of the team met for pizza. I ate and drove back here."

Beth's brows drew together. "That's it?"

"Boring, huh?"

"Well, yes. He didn't ask you out?"

"I don't know why he would."

Beth stopped what she was doing. "Your unfinished business in Sheridan? I don't get the sense either of you is over your relationship before he moved to Idaho."

"Well, he doesn't seem to have an interest in me other than as a friend. It's better this way. Especially if I'm ever accepted into one of the culinary programs." She blew out a shaky laugh. "Then I'd be the one moving away."

Beth didn't believe her, deciding to keep the doubt to herself. "You may be right. Relationships aren't easy."

Setting a tray on the counter, Beth added the cups of coffee, packets of sugar, and individual cream containers. "Be right back."

Abigail let out a relieved breath. She didn't want to think about Quinn. Nor did she want to talk about Mason, which would've been Beth's next topic.

She hadn't heard from him since Friday night. Didn't expect to. Not sure she'd answer the phone if he did call. The way Mason had looked at the other woman told Abigail he had a genuine interest in her.

"Okay, the men are set for now." Beth slid the tray back into its spot, returning to breakfast preparations. Glancing at the clock, she picked up her pace. "The ranch hands should be filing in soon."

The words had just left her mouth when voices floated into the kitchen from the dining room. "There are pastries and coffee already set out," Abigail said when she saw Beth tense. "They'll be fine until the rest of this is ready."

"Did Lydia provide the pastries?"

"They were in the freezer."

"Oh, right."

Scooping the eggs into a warmed servicing dish, Abigail stilled at the familiar voice coming from the dining room.

"I forgot to tell you. Quinn decided to come down for breakfast with the consultant he and Jake are using."

"You mean for expanding their herd?"

"Right. Jake is already convinced we should breed Wagyu beef. They're working on the details." Sliding cooked bacon and sausage onto a platter, Beth took them and the eggs to the dining room.

Abigail finished buttering toast when the door opened. Expecting to see Beth, she was surprised at the sight of Quinn holding a cup of coffee.

"Good morning, Abbie."

"Quinn."

"Thought I'd check to see if you'd like to ride together to practice on Friday? We'll probably go to the same pizza place afterward." He blew across the dark liquid before taking a tentative sip.

"I don't know..."

"No use both of us driving. I could pick you up at six-thirty."

Hesitating, she searched for a polite way to decline. "I may not want pizza afterward. It would be best if I drove."

"If you don't want to meet the others, I'll bring you back to the ranch. Totally up to you."

Riding together did make sense. Plus, she was low on gas. "Oh, all right. If you change your mind, let me know."

"I won't change my mind, Abbie. See you Friday."

Abigail waited outside on Friday for Quinn to pick her up. She'd called him half a dozen times to cancel, hanging up before he answered. It seemed such an immature act over a shared ride to softball practice. Afterall, it wasn't as if they'd be spending hours alone together.

She heard Quinn's truck before seeing it. Inhaling a deep breath, Abigail exhaled as he stopped beside her. Climbing in, she shot him a quick glance while securing the seatbelt, then looked up at the sky.

"They're calling for rain."

Quinn continued to the highway. "I know. Let's hope it comes after we're finished with practice."

Falling into an easy banter, Abigail couldn't help recalling how effortless their conversations used to be. By the time they arrived at the community park, she found herself laughing at a story Quinn told.

When practice ended, several people asked Abigail if she'd be joining everyone at the pizza place. Her initial thought had been to decline, using the excuse about how early she had to rise to get breakfast ready.

"Yes. I rode with Quinn, so it's up to him."

"If Quinn isn't going, you can ride with me, Abbie." Blake stood next to her.

"She's riding with me." Quinn took a spot on the other side of Abigail, glancing down at her. "Are you ready?"

Nodding, Abigail did her best to hide a grin. "Just need to pack my gear."

It took little time for her to stow her equipment. As she did, her gaze wandered to where Quinn and Blake stood together, talking in low tones no one else could hear.

The pizza parlor was already full with several teams who'd been practicing at the community fields. Quinn spotted their group right away, following Barrel's voice to their table. Leaving to place their order, he took a spot behind Sam.

From her spot at the table, she watched the two joke around, laughing at what the other said. Sam seemed to take every opportunity to touch Quinn. Not in intimate ways, but familiar, as if they were good friends. Which puzzled her.

Quinn worked for Jake, while Sam spent her time at Whistle Rock Ranch. Abigail didn't know when they'd had time to build a friendship.

"Hey, Abbie. What did you think of practice?" Owen stood beside her, a soda in one hand. Married with two children, everyone liked and respected him.

"We've improved since last week. I'm glad Virgil is acting as the manager. He may not have played in high school or college, but he knows the game."

Glancing at the order counter, her chest tightened at seeing Quinn's hand on Sam's shoulder. Maybe they were closer than she thought.

"The season starts in two weeks. What do you think of having a second practice on Sunday afternoons?"

Abigail shifted her attention from Quinn to Owen. "Sundays are fine with me, as long as Beth doesn't need me."

"Great. Virgil's been polling everyone. So far, everyone is good with it. There'd be one the day after tomorrow and another next Sunday. I'll let Virg know."

"Sure," Abigail responded, though her mind was elsewhere.

She reminded herself Quinn hadn't expressed an interest in her as more than a friend. Perhaps he'd decided to move on. The idea saddened her.

Returning to her spot at the table, she waited for Quinn to return with the drinks. She wouldn't let on her appetite had vanished.

"Here we are. The pizza should be ready in a few minutes." He set down a soda for her and beer for him. "I ordered it with everything. Hope that was all right."

"Perfect."

Instead of sitting beside her, his large, strong hands rested on her shoulders and began to knead. "You seem real tight tonight, Abbie. Anything bothering you?"

"Uh, no. Everything is fine." The lie tasted bitter in her mouth. Closing her eyes, she let him work his magic. Muscles she hadn't realized were tense relaxed under his touch.

"Large everything pizza?"

"That's us." Quinn stopped the massage, taking a seat beside her. Selecting a piece with lots of sausage and mushrooms, he set it on her plate. "There you go."

Before she could thank him, Quinn leaned toward her, brushing a kiss across her cheek. The gesture made her gasp. Glancing around, she let out a breath when seeing no one was paying any attention to them.

"What was that for?"

Soft, emerald green eyes bore into hers. "I wanted you to know how much you still mean to me." Touching her hand with his, he leaned closer. "And it was a warning."

Licking her lips, she exhaled a sigh. "A warning?"

A slow smile appeared on his face. "Be warned, Abigail Kelman. I love you, and I'm going to do all I can to convince you how good we are together."

Chapter Twelve

Abigail piled sandwiches on a tray, adding bunches of grapes and orange slices. "Beth, would you mind bringing the salad and bowls. They already have drinks and silverware."

"Sure."

Entering Wyatt's office, Abigail nodded at the men scattered throughout the room. Aiden Winters had returned after doing his own research into the Nielson brothers. He sat next to Blake, both acting as if they were good friends.

Setting down the tray, she noticed their glasses were still full. "Let me know if you want anything else."

Returning to the kitchen, men's voices drew her to the window. Anson, Gage, and Jonah Bonner stood about fifteen feet away from the kitchen door. Gage used his hands to describe something, Anson shaking his head as his face reddened.

"What are you looking at?" Beth moved to stand beside her. "Those three have been going at it on and off for a couple hours. Since about the time we started lunch prep."

"What are they talking about?" Abigail turned her head to see if she could pick up the conversation.

"Anson had never liked the idea of a dude ranch. He's been lobbying to get out of the business and concentrate on cattle and horses. As you'd expect, he's alone in the argument."

"But he owns the ranch."

"He and Margie, and she's one hundred percent behind the guest ranch concept. Instead of accepting he's lost the argument, Anson keeps bringing it up. Margie's afraid he's going to work himself up until he has another heart attack. I told her to get him away from the ranch, maybe go on a cruise to Europe this time."

Abigail faced her. "Let me guess. Margie's concerned about being away right before the dude ranch opens for the season."

"Exactly. I understand, though. The thing is, she has an experienced group of people who can take over while they're gone. She should take advantage of the fact and get out of here while Anson's still healthy enough to travel."

"You don't think..." Abigail frowned as her voice trailed off.

"He's had one bad heart attack. You just never know."

Before either woman could return to their work, a shout came from outside. Turning back to the window, they saw three men enter the corral. A moment later, they dragged another man through the gate, where others gathered around them.

"Can you see who it is?"

Abigail moved to the door. "No, but I'm going to find out." She tossed her apron on the counter before rushing outside.

Anson, Gage, and Jonah were almost to the corral when sirens sounded. Glancing over her shoulder, Abigail saw an emergency truck and the sheriff's SUV pull into the ranch. She slipped next to Owen.

"Who is it?"

"Brady."

"Virgil's cousin?"

"Right. Got thrown and landed wrong." Owen shook his head. "He hasn't moved since he hit the ground."

Virgil pushed past everyone, rushing into the corral ahead of the EMTs. Dropping to his knees, he looked up and down his cousin's prone body. He didn't see any obvious injuries, which didn't mean anything.

"Brady, can you hear me?"

"Sir, we'll need you to move aside." The EMT got a good look at the man kneeling on the ground. "Is that you, Virgil?"

"Yeah. Brady's my cousin. Got thrown from a horse he was breaking."

"We'll take good care of him. Please move so I can do my job."

Twenty minutes passed before the EMTs loaded Brady into the ambulance. Virgil followed in his truck, Wyatt in the passenger seat.

Watching them leave, the mood at the ranch turned somber. Jasper and Monica Redstar had followed in their truck, with Anson and Margie right behind them, leaving Jake in charge of the ranch hands.

Gathering everyone together, he waited until the sirens had faded into the distance. "I know you're worried about Brady. Virgil will let us know how he's doing as soon as the doctors know anything. I'd appreciate it if you'd get back to what you were doing."

Jake called Quinn as everyone dispersed. "There's a problem here at the ranch. Virgil's cousin, Brady, was thrown from a horse. He didn't come to before the EMTs arrived. The bosses are at the hospital, so I've got to stay here."

"No problem. I've got everything here covered. Let me know how Brady's doing."

"Will do." Ending the call, Jake headed to the kitchen. "Hey, sweetheart." Nodding at Abigail, he swiped a cookie from a cooling rack. "You heard about Brady?"

Beth stopped what she was doing to nod. "Yes. Have you heard anything?"

"Not yet. It may be a while. I've let Quinn know. I could end up staying in the bunkhouse with the rest of the ranch hands."

"Don't worry about having to stay. I have my car," Beth said. "Be sure to update us on Brady."

Virgil called Jake at midnight, tired and stressed. The call lasted no more than five minutes, yet it left the foreman with a sick sensation in his stomach. Calling Beth, his message hadn't been a good one.

"Brady has a concussion, broken leg, and bruised kidney. The doctors had stabilized him. All had gone well until he was given penicillin. He immediately experienced anaphylaxis."

"Oh, no. How is he now?"

"The symptoms developed right away. The doctor administered epinephrine, which stabilized Brady. A scary situation. I don't know how long they'll keep him in the hospital. Virgil's going to stay the night. Anson, Margie, and Wyatt are heading back to the ranch. I'm going to wait until they get back, then I'll drive home."

"I'll wait up."

"If you can sleep, do it, Beth. Love you."

"Love you, too."

Resting his arms on his thighs, Jake hung his head to stare at the bunkroom floor. One of his best men, Brady, never complained, working twice as hard as many of the ranch hands.

He'd witnessed plenty of ranch accidents over the years, most resulting in a full recovery. A few had caused more permanent damage. Jake sent up a short prayer Brady would fall into the first category.

"What did you hear, boss?"

Jake lifted his head to see Barrel in front of him. While explaining, several other ranch hands joined them. Seemed no one had been able to sleep without word on Brady.

"With the penicillin situation controlled, the docs will concentrate on the concussion and kidney."

"How soon will he be back at the ranch, Jake?" Barrel asked.

"I don't know. Wyatt is driving back to the ranch with his parents. He may know more. My guess is it's too soon for the doctors to predict."

Grave expressions and slow nods preceded the men walking back to their beds. Jake doubted anyone would get much sleep. Their concern underscored by Jake staying at Whistle Rock Ranch. The ranch hands were close, had formed friendships deeper than any he'd seen at other ranches. He figured a lot of prayers would be voiced that night.

The weather continued to warm over the two weeks Brady stayed in the hospital. The men spoke of him often, most visited at least once. Brady never said much, which surprised no one. A quiet man by nature, he was friendly, keeping private matters to himself.

Over those two weeks, Abigail saw Quinn at practices, had been disappointed when he hadn't invited her to ride with him. Once, he brought his friend and Wagyu beef consultant, Benny Takada.

Quinn had been cordial, showing none of the closeness of a couple weeks earlier. She didn't know what had changed. Perhaps it had to do with Benny's presence. Abigail suspected the reason was more simple. In his mind, they were friends and nothing more.

A lowkey celebration had been planned for Brady's return. Abigail and Beth planned the food while Margie and Monica put up a few decorations in the bunkhouse.

When Virgil and Wyatt arrived with Brady, everyone stopped what they were doing. Gathering around the truck, they applauded and whooped when the passenger door opened. Owen and Barrel stepped forward to help him, but Brady shook his head, determined to use the crutches to walk on his own.

Abigail watched from where she stood on the kitchen stoop. Jake must have called Quinn, because he arrived a few minutes later to welcome Brady. The two spoke a minute or so before the recovering ranch hand took a seat outside the bunkhouse. Abigail suspected he wanted to spend as much time as possible outside, soaking up the clean air and sunshine.

Quinn joined Jake and Virgil, their gazes moving to Brady and over the gathering. She saw the instant he spotted her, a slow smile appearing on his face. He said a few words to the others before walking to stand next to her.

"Hey."

"Hey yourself," she replied, her attention still on Brady. "How is he doing?"

"Virgil says he's ready to go back to work. Brady told me the same. The doctor who released him warned he needed to take it easy and not push too hard. The broken leg limits what he can do."

"So he doesn't have much choice but to take it easy."

Quinn chuckled. "Right. Virgil had assigned men to take turns hanging with Brady until the leg heals."

"He'll figure out what's going on the first day."

"Yeah, but there's no real choice. The Bonners support Virgil, and what the bosses say goes." Quinn shoved his hands in his back pockets, making no move to leave.

A few minutes into the silence, Abigail cleared her throat. "How have you been?"

"Good. Busy. Benny left a week ago to do some negotiating for us."

Brows scrunched, she stared up at him. "Negotiating?"

"Seeing what we'll have to spend to start the new venture. We'll need a bull and several cows, plus additional fencing to keep them separate from the Angus cattle. Those are the most important outlays."

"Can Jake afford it?"

"He says he can." Searching the crowd, he spotted Sam. "I need to talk to someone before heading back. Can you get the time off to have dinner with me on Saturday?"

The invitation surprised her. "What time?"

"Seven?"

"I doubt it will be a problem."

"Great."

"Casual?"

"I'll let you know when I decide where we're going. See you Saturday."

He walked straight to Sam before she could respond.

Chapter Thirteen

Abigail stayed busy the following days through work and anger at Quinn for leaving her to spend time with Sam. What was it about the ranch hand that drew him to her?

As irritated as she was at Quinn, she told herself not to worry about the attention he paid to Sam. She was having dinner with him Saturday night, not the female ranch hand.

"What's got you so riled up?" Beth poured batter into a large, flat cakepan, smoothing the mixture outward before sliding it into the oven.

"What are you talking about?"

"You've been slamming pans onto the counter. And you should check the mixing bowl, as there could be a crack up the side."

Grabbing the bowl from the counter, Abigail rotated it while looking for damage. Setting it down, she rested a hand on the edge of the counter.

"Sorry. I didn't realize..."

"So, what is bothering you?"

"It's nothing," Abigail muttered, almost too low for Beth to hear.

"Gotta be something. You might as well tell me."

Biting her lower lip, Abigail released a sigh. "It's Quinn."

"Okay."

"He asked me to dinner on Saturday. I said yes, assuming I can get off early."

"We can work it out. So, why are you upset?"

Abigail rubbed both hands down her apron. "It's silly."

Crossing her arms, Beth leaned a hip against a counter. "It's not silly if it bothers you this much."

"What do you think of Sam?"

"Are you talking about the ranch hand?"

Abigail nodded. "Yes."

"Well, Jake says she's one of the best people he has." Beth tapped a finger against her lips. "Let's see. She's always in a good mood, never complains, and does the work of more than one person. Why are you asking?"

Shaking her head, she rubbed a hand across her forehead. "I don't know. It's just... Well...it's just that Quinn spends a lot of time with her. Whenever he comes here, you can find him with her. Same with softball practice. The last practice, he had his friend, Benny, in the truck. They stopped here to pick up Sam. He usually asks me if I want a ride. Not that time. It just seemed odd."

Dropping her arms to her sides, Beth poured herself a cup of coffee. "I've never noticed him pay Sam any particular attention. I do know Quinn feels the same about her as Jake. In fact, they'd like to lure her to our ranch, but don't want to upset the Bonners."

"Oh."

"Yeah. We need at least one more ranch hand, and will be looking for another one when the new program starts."

"The Wagyu beef must require a considerable amount of money."

"A lot. It's good Jake has been setting most of his earnings aside for a long time. I've done the same, but not nearly as much as what he's stashed away. Anyway, I wouldn't put too much energy into worrying about Sam. You're the one he asked to dinner. That's a much bigger signal."

"You think so?"

"Absolutely."

"You could be right. Thanks, Beth."

"Anytime you want to talk, you know where to find me. Let's finish up here and figure out Saturday." Beth smiled. "We'll get all the prep done early so you have time to clean up and get dressed."

Checking the mirror one last time, Abigail picked up her purse and coat. On a final thought, she lifted a hat from its hook by the door of her apartment. Taking a deep breath, she let it out slowly before opening the door.

She didn't know why her heart pounded while butterflies took residence in her stomach. How many times had she and Quinn gone out for dinner? Too many for this to be affecting her so much. At least that's what she told herself while walking back into the kitchen.

"Is there anything I can do until Quinn arrives?"

"Nope." Beth set a tray aside. "Everything is ready to be set out. You look great, Abbie."

"Thanks. Quinn called to tell me it's casual but to dress warm. He says there's a minor cold front coming through."

"Jake stopped by to tell me the same. When will Quinn get here?"

"Any minute." The kitchen door opened as Abigail finished answering. Quinn walked in looking like a GQ model. Clean jeans, dark gray long-sleeved shirt, black boots, and a gray cowboy hat.

"Hope I'm not late." Removing the hat, he ran fingers through his hair. "You look fantastic, Abbie."

Feeling her face heat, she glanced away before meeting his gaze. "Thank you. You look real good yourself."

"Thanks. Are you ready to go?"

"Yes. See you tomorrow, Beth."

Quinn had parked the truck as close to the lodge as possible. Feeling the chill in the air, she slipped into her coat before claiming her seat. They were on their way a few minutes later.

He shot her a look. "How has your week gone?"

"Good. Beth and I have a routine, which helps. What about you?"

"Busy, but good. Jake has made the decision to go forward with purchasing what's needed to start offering Wagyu beef. We're fencing off areas for when the bull and cows arrive."

"When will that be?"

"Two weeks."

Her eyes widened, surprised at the speed of the change. "Why so fast?"

"Jake wants to have everything together before the bad weather hits in the fall. He and Benny believe all the cows will be ready to drop calves next spring."

She clasped her hands in her lap. "It will take a year before the first calves arrive, then how long before they're mature?"

"Around thirty months. They're a little slower to mature than other breeds, such as Angus." Quinn's voice held an edge of excitement. "They also take a little more care than American breeds. You can see why Jake wants to get started as soon as possible."

"I know this means a great deal to you."

"Yeah, it does. It's fulfilling to introduce something new into what a rancher offers. We're fortunate to be in a geographic market which craves a higher grade of beef." Staring ahead, he gave a slow shake of his head. "Enough about what I'm doing. Any new responsibilities?"

"Not really. Honestly, I'm not even sure what else I could be doing. She lets me create menus, order supplies, and take the lead on the main dish. I've also come up with some appetizers. Unfortunately, we don't prepare them except for special dinners or parties. Beth is pretty unusual. Most chefs keep a tight control."

"Maybe because it's just the two of you?"

She chuckled. "Probably." Watching the scenery, she shifted toward him. "Where are we going?"

"I heard about a new Italian restaurant in Castle Rock." Quinn mentioned a small town between Brilliance and Jackson. "How does that sound?"

"Excellent. I love all varieties of pasta. I'm trying to convince Beth to add more Italian items to our revolving menu." Focusing out the front window, Abigail noticed small flakes of snow slapping against the front of the truck.

"Guess the storm front is arriving faster than I anticipated." Quinn slowed down as the scattered snow became consistent flakes against the windshield. He checked the time. They were about twenty minutes north of Castle Rock.

Neither spoke as the storm worsened. Quinn slowed further when visibility became almost zero. He thought of the storm a few weeks earlier, forcing him and Abigail to stop over at a motel for a few hours.

"I think it's getting worse." Abigail leaned forward in an attempt to see better. "I can't make out more than a few feet in front of us." She continued to be a second set of eyes for Quinn, who also strained to see ahead. "This might be worse than the other storm."

"You may be right." His knuckles whitened as his hands tightened on the steering wheel. "Look for a place we can turn off."

"The road drops off a little bit on this side. As I recall, it's about two feet. Maybe there will be a road we can use."

Quinn hoped the storm would pass by, providing an open view to the road ahead. It didn't happen. A strong wind joined the snowstorm, reducing his vision even more.

He crept along at less than ten miles per hour on a road meant for much higher speeds.

"Look there." Abigail's voice rose as she pointed ahead. "I'm pretty sure that's a road to the right."

"Good eyes, Abbie." Slowing to a crawl, Quinn almost stopped to confirm what she'd seen was a road. Turning the wheel to the right, he continued forward a few feet at a time. "Seems solid." Satisfied they were off the road, he parked, still hopeful the storm would pass.

"How long do you think we'll have to stay here?"

Reaching over, he covered her hand with his. "I have no idea. At least we have plenty of water. There are blankets in the back seat and some protein bars."

"Guess I should've worn warmer clothes." She scooted closer to Quinn.

"We're going to be fine. There is plenty of gas, so I'll leave the engine running for a while. Let's get in the back seat so we can sit next to each other."

Climbing into the back, he held out his hands to help Abigail. Once settled, he reached under the seat, pulling out three blankets.

"I keep these in the truck year-round. These spring storms are often unexpected and deadly."

They spread the blankets over them, tucking close to each other. "I can't believe we've been stranded by two storms. We weren't stranded even once in Sheridan." She smiled at him, softening her words.

He settled an arm over her shoulders, tugging her against him. "Guess we're just lucky."

Pulling his phone out of the pocket of his coat, he grimaced. "No service."

"Did you expect there'd be?"

Chuckling, he slipped the phone away. "One can hope."

"Yes. There's always hope."

Studying her face, he saw the fear in her eyes. Tightening his arm around her, he kissed her forehead.

"We're going to be all right. It may take time, but we will get out of here, Abbie."

"Pinky swear?"

Laughing, he held up a hand. "Absolutely."

Chapter Fourteen

Abigail blinked several times, then sat up. Recalling the storm, she stared at the blanket wrapped around her. A quick glance to her side gave her a start.

Quinn, leaning against the door on his side of the truck, met her gaze. "Hello, princess."

She choked out a laugh while running fingers through disheveled locks of hair. "I'm hardly a princess. What time is it?" Judging by the snow falling, the storm had slowed.

"Just before midnight. It's clear enough to drive back to the ranch."

"I'm starving."

"So am I, Abbie. If you know of a place open this late, I'm happy to drive there." Tossing off the blanket, he climbed into the front seat. The engine started right up.

Abigail followed him, though she pulled the blanket behind her. Spreading it over her legs, she smiled.

"There's a Mexican takeout place in Jackson, but that's probably an hour away."

"Open twenty-four-seven?"

"Yep. I can check as soon we get phone service."

"Then let's get to Jackson."

Quinn pulled onto the highway. "You fell asleep about fifteen minutes after closing your eyes."

"Did you sleep?"

"I wanted to stay awake in case there was an opening in the storm."

She remembered the hesitancy in his voice. "And?"

"Right. In case we attracted visitors."

Abigail had read about roaming thieves who preyed on stranded travelers in the area around Brilliance. There'd been no deaths reported, though several people had been beaten when refusing to hand over valuables.

"Smart. Did you see anyone?"

Quinn shook his head. "No one. Maybe they've moved on."

"Or they couldn't see us due to the storm."

Settling against the seat, Abigail stared out the window. Unlike during the storm, she could see lights burning inside nearby residences.

"Are you still seeing the doctor?"

Quinn's question surprised her. "Not anymore."

"Why not?"

Shifting in the seat, she crossed her arms. "I should say it's none of your business."

"But?"

A slow grin tipped up the corners of her mouth. "It's no real secret. Mason is dating his real estate agent. Or he was when he stood me up for a date in order to share a movie and pizza with her."

"Stood you up?"

"Technically, he called to say the hospital needed him to take another shift."

"How'd you find out?" Quinn slowed to avoid a fallen tree limb.

"They were at the pizza parlor our first night of practice."

"What a rotten move."

"Yeah, it was."

Glancing toward her, he grinned. "Want me to beat him up?"

Laughing, she shook her head. "No. The real estate agent dumped him because he pulled the same on her. She found him with one of the nurses at the hospital on an evening they were supposed to have dinner. Guess he's a serial dumper."

"Dumper?"

"You know. A man who dates a woman a few times, then moves on without telling her it's over."

"So the doc is a coward."

"I don't know what he is. What about you?"

"Me, what, Abbie?"

"Are you dating anyone?"

He thought a moment. "I'm hoping it's you."

"Me? As I recall, we've already done that, and it didn't work out so well."

"My fault," he interjected quickly.

Staring at the hand in his lap, she reached over, placing her hand on top. "Both of us were at fault, Quinn."

Feeling the warmth of her hand on his, he nodded. "You may be right."

Abigail finished the last of the preparations for the ranch's Sunday breakfast, her mind on the night before. A grin brightened her features when she recalled the instant the Mexican restaurant came into view. Quinn had let out an impressive whoop when spotting the open sign.

Except for the occasional vehicle in the drive-through, they'd been the only patrons. Abigail had eaten her chicken enchiladas with gusto, the same as Quinn had tucked into his carnitas burrito and chili relleno. She chuckled, remembering his reaction to the food.

"This is great." He'd picked up a glass filled with Jarritos mandarin soda, washing down a large bite of burrito.

"What's so funny, Abbie?" Beth closed the refrigerator door.

For a few minutes, she'd forgotten about standing in the ranch kitchen. "Thinking about last night."

"Jake and I noticed Quinn returning fairly late. The storm hold you up?"

"For a few hours. We had to pull off the road and wait until it passed."

"Did you ever get dinner?"

Abigail placed the last batch of bacon into a serving tray, setting the cover on top. "Do you remember Humberto's?"

Beth's brow rose. "The drive-through Mexican place?"

"That's the one. They were the only place open."

"How was it?" Beth used a whisk to blend the eggs and milk in a large bowl.

"Great. I had chicken enchiladas, which were excellent. Quinn gave me a bite of his carnitas burrito. I expected the pulled pork to be dry, but it was moist. And the seasoning was perfect."

"I'm guessing you were starving."

"Well, yes. Still, the food was much better than expected." Abigail moved the bacon with slices of ham on the griddle before mixing the pancake batter. "Are we adding anything to the pancakes today?"

Beth shook her head. "Let's go with half plain and half blueberry. Those are the most popular." Setting the egg mixture aside, she faced Abigail. "Did you two talk about what happened?"

She knew what Beth meant. "Honestly, we talked little about him leaving Sheridan for Idaho. He did ask me to dinner next Saturday. And he plans to come for Sunday dinner tonight."

"Sounds to me as if he's angling for a second chance."

Abigail smiled at the comment. "Yes, I believe you're right."

"And you?"

She began cooking the pancakes, setting the bowl aside. "I believe a second chance is a very good idea."

Quinn encouraged his ranch hands to do minimal chores on Sunday before church, taking the rest of the day to relax. Most weekends, they did. As foreman, he wasn't in a position to let his chores go.

Standing outside the barn, he made a slow circle, gauging what he had to accomplish. There wasn't much. The ranch hands had done more than their share before kicking back.

Deciding nothing required his attention outside, he headed into the house. There were calls he needed to make, and he planned to review the latest numbers Benny had prepared.

As was his habit, he called his parents first. They talked for almost an hour, first with his mother, then his father.

Similar to Trace Griffin's parents, his father still ran cattle on his own ranch. In their early fifties, his parents planned to work several more years. He knew his father wanted him to return some day to run the ranch. Maybe he would. For now, his time was better spent learning as much as possible about breeding Wagyu beef.

Before calling Benny, he read through the documents his friend had forwarded. The numbers were good, better than Quinn and Jake expected.

Grabbing a pen, he circled sections he wanted Benny to clarify. Flipping to another page, he checked the column of numbers once more. Adding Wagyu to the ranch could be a profitable investment.

As with all ranching operations, success hinged on the weather, cost of feed, illness, and shrinkage due to factors ranging from attacks by predators to cattle rustling. The latter was more prevalent than most people realized.

Though ranchers took precautions, rustlers had grown smarter at isolating groups of cattle. They were quick, rounding up the animals before herding them into waiting semitrailers.

A major deterrent to stealing from Jake's ranch centered on his decision to tag and brand his Angus cattle, the same as the previous ranch owner. Quinn agreed with his boss's decision. There'd been no loss of cattle from the ranch in over ten years. However, it had to remain on the list of items which could impact the cost of raising cattle for market.

Tapping Benny's phone number, they exchanged pleasantries and schedules before getting to Quinn's questions. Jotting down the answers, they ended the call an hour later.

Shoving back his chair, he scrubbed a hand over his face. Quinn felt good. He saw no obstacles to adding Wagyu beef.

Deciding coffee sounded good, he made his way to the kitchen. Beth was at Whistle Rock Ranch, and Jake had traveled to an auction a few hours north, leaving the house to himself. While waiting for coffee to fill his cup, he checked the refrigerator. He pulled out leftover ham and beef, along with mustard and mayonnaise.

Opening the pantry door, he reached for a loaf of bread when a knock on the front door stopped him. Quinn hesitated a moment. Jake and Beth rarely had visitors.

When the knock sounded again, he closed the pantry door. "I'm coming."

He opened the front door, his gaze landing on a man dressed similar to him, the cowboy hat concealing most of his face. "What can I do for you?"

"I'm looking for Quinn Sawyer."

"You found him."

The visitor fell silent for several seconds. Just when Quinn had decided to ask what the man wanted, he lifted his head.

Quinn's body tensed at what he saw. The man's eyes, his nose, the set of his jaw. A younger version of Quinn. His hand fisted at his side. His voice lowered to a controlled growl.

"Who are you?"

The visitor looked around before locking his emerald green eyes with Quinn's. They were the same color, same intensity, as the man who stood inside the house.

"May I come inside?"

"Not until you tell me who you are." Quinn's hand opened, then closed once more into a fist.

"My name is Logan. Logan Sawyer. I'm your half-brother."

Chapter Fifteen

Quinn fought the immediate urge to grab the stranger by his collar and toss him off the porch. Flexing his fingers several times, he sucked in a deep breath, slowly exhaling. Voice hard, he glared at the interloper.

"Say...that...again."

Face tight, the visitor put more distance between them, his response clipped. "I'm Logan Sawyer, your half-brother. Wallace Sawyer is my father." When Quinn didn't respond, he continued. "I know this is a shock. When I found out Pop, uh...Wallace, had another family, I landed a blow to his face."

"You hit him?"

"I did. What he and my mother did was reprehensible."

"When was this?"

"Last summer. July, I believe."

Closing his eyes, Quinn forced down the bile lodged in his throat. "I remember asking him what happened to his face. He shrugged it off without answering." Drawing the door wider, he motioned Logan inside. "Come on in."

His half-brother stopped midway into the living room, looking around. "This your place?"

"No. It belongs to Jake and Beth Kelman. I'm the foreman."

Logan nodded, his expression inscrutable.

"Do you want coffee, water, a beer?"

"Water would be good. Thanks." He followed Quinn into the kitchen.

Handing him a bottle, Quinn indicated a chair. "Sit down and tell me everything."

Logan hesitated a moment before lowering himself into one of the chairs around a wood table. Unscrewing the cap, he drank half the bottle before setting it down.

"It's not complicated. Our father had an affair with my mother, Claudia. She was younger, single. To be honest, she set her sights on Wallace."

"Set her sights, huh?"

"That's her wording. At the time, you were about six, your sister wasn't born yet. She thought he'd fall in love with her and leave your mother." Logan shook his head in disgust. "Wallace had no intention of leaving your mother. It's just me. No siblings. Mother never married. Wallace stopped coming around to see her about the time I turned four. Afterward, he came once every other week to see me. You know, trying to be a real father." Shrugging, he grabbed the bottle of water, swallowing the rest of the contents. "That's really all there is to it."

Quinn continued to stare at a specific gouge in the table, fighting to accept Logan's words. All those years, he'd never had a clue.

"You're saying our father saw your mother from the time I was six until I was ten?"

"He saw her for about five years. I think Mother said you were eleven. To be clear, she never expressed any regret at having the affair. She wanted Wallace and went after him, unconcerned about how it would affect you or your mother."

"Does my mother know?"

"It's doubtful. If she did, I'm pretty sure it would be obvious."

Quinn blew out a breath. "Yeah." Standing, he walked to a window, pulling back the draperies to look outside. "What do you want?"

"I don't know exactly. Guess I wanted to meet my big brother."

Whirling back to face Logan, he crossed his arms. "Well, you've met me. Now what?"

Rising, he shrugged as if disappointed, but resigned. Blowing out a breath, he headed to the front door. Quinn's question stopped him from walking out.

"Where are you going?"

"I haven't decided. My goal was to meet you. I hadn't planned much beyond that."

Quinn let his gaze wander over Logan. "Have you ever worked with cattle?"

"A little. Pop...our father...got me a job with a local rancher when I was sixteen. The last six years I've been working in construction."

"No college?"

Logan looked down at his boots, shaking his head. "No money. Which was okay."

"Did Wallace pay your mother anything?"

"When he could. Mom worked as a receptionist for a law firm, and three evenings a week at a diner outside of Sheridan. She stopped the evening work when I graduated from high school. That's when I got a job working with a neighbor who owned a construction firm. A room in his house came with the job, so..." He shrugged again.

Dropping his arms to his sides, Quinn stepped away from the window. "Are you looking for work?"

"Always."

Quinn chuckled. "We're going to be hiring in the next few weeks. Nothing glamorous, base pay, but it comes with a place to stay. The bunkhouse here is real nice. Are you interested?"

His face slackened in surprise. "I am. Don't you want to call people I've worked for, or my mother?"

Quinn stared at him long enough to make a decision. "I'm going to talk to our father."

Quinn spent the rest of the day showing Logan around the ranch. Each talked about their past without the rancor each expected.

"Afterall," Quinn had said. "It's not our fault Wallace and your mother made a decision to cheat. Who I feel bad about is my mother. She's the real victim."

Logan had agreed not to tell his mother about meeting Quinn. Neither of the brothers wanted word getting back to Wallace before Quinn was ready to contact him.

By the time the sun dropped behind the western mountain range, both were starving. The refrigerator held leftover lasagna, chicken piccata, and roast beef, all from dinners at Whistle Rock Ranch.

Quinn had taken his last bite when the front door opened. Shoving back his chair, he froze at the look on Beth's face.

"Did you forget about dinner with Abigail?"

His face fell. Standing, he grabbed the empty plate and glass. "I'd better find Abigail and explain."

Beth's attention switched to the man still sitting at the table. Logan almost jumped out of his chair.

"Ma'am."

"I don't believe we've met."

"No, ma'am, we haven't. I'm Logan Sawyer."

"He's my half-brother, Beth. We met for the first time today. If you and Jake approve, he'll be working here."

"Half-brother, huh? Well, I can see why Quinn forgot about dinner. Nice to meet you, Logan."

"Pleasure's mine, ma'am. I'll clean up the kitchen and get to the bunkhouse."

Beth held out a covered dish. "Before you go, there's leftover pie. It would go well with a cup of coffee."

Logan slashed a glance at Quinn, who nodded. "That would be real nice, ma'am."

"Great. But there's one condition. No more ma'am. Please call me Beth."

Face reddening, he nodded. "I can do that."

"I'll save enough for you, Quinn. Jake made it back to Whistle Rock Ranch early. He's already eaten. In fact, he's in the barn and wants to speak with you."

"I'll talk to him before finding Abigail." Walking toward the living room, he stopped next to Logan. "See you in the morning."

"Definitely. And thanks, Quinn."

Giving a curt nod, he grabbed his hat before leaving to talk with Jake and locate Abigail.

Quinn saw her through the kitchen window before entering through the back door. "Hello, Abbie."

She didn't respond, but continued packaging the small amount of food left from dinner. When finished, she labeled the package, setting it on a shelf in one of the freezers.

Joining her, he leaned down. "I'm sorry. Something important came up and I couldn't get here. I should've called."

"It would've been nice."

Wrapping an arm around her, he kissed her forehead. "Have you eaten?"

"Yes. I haven't had dessert, though."

"Is there enough to share?"

"Yes. I'll make coffee." Voice frosty, she at least was talking to him.

They shared the table in the kitchen, Abigail's body language letting him know she wasn't quite mollified. He waited until she took a bite of pie and swallowed some coffee before talking.

"A stranger showed up today. His name is Logan Sawyer."

She stopped with the fork partway to her mouth. "Sawyer?"

"Claims to be my half-brother."

Setting her fork down, she leaned toward him. "But that would mean..." Her voice faded.

"Yeah. Logan says we have the same father."

"Wow. He had an affair?"

"According to Logan, his mother and my father had an affair when I was about six. It continued for five years before he ended it." He stared at the slice of pie, no longer hungry. Pushing the plate away, he ran a hand over his face. "Mom doesn't know."

Scooting her chair closer, she placed a hand on his arm. "I'm sorry, Quinn. It's got to be a huge shock."

"It is. I've always looked up to Pop. Never could've imagined him cheating on Mom."

"What are you going to do?"

Lifting his cup, he drank the now tepid coffee. "I plan to talk to him. I'm going to give it a few days, maybe longer. The best would be to confront him face-to-face."

"Jake won't have an issue with you leaving for a few days."

His chuckle held no humor. "I don't plan to be gone more than a day. I'll drive to Sheridan in the morning and return after we talk."

"What about your mother? It will kill Sally to learn what Wallace did. The fact he kept it up for so many years. I don't know, Quinn. If it were me, I'd find it hard to trust him again."

Rubbing his forehead with shaky fingers, he stared at her hand on his arm. "I'm so angry at him, Abbie. It would be different if it was a one-time thing. But five years?" His voice rose on the last. "I hope Mom never finds out."

They sat in silence for several minutes without talking. Quinn's jaw worked as he let the truth sink in. He'd thought talking it out with Logan would've softened the fury he felt at his father's betrayal.

"Do you want me to go with you?"

Her offer meant a great deal to him. "I appreciate it, Abbie, but this is something I have to do alone."

Chapter Sixteen

Quinn tightened the fence wire while Logan secured it in place. They'd been fixing fences for the last couple days, after setting up several corrals for the shipment expected the following week. Given what had to be done regarding their father, they'd accomplished more than expected.

Both had been mulling over when was best for Quinn to confront Wallace. Neither felt an urgency to stir up trouble after all these years. And the discussion would result in trouble.

Wallace Sawyer had a temper, though it started as a slow simmer before erupting. The brothers expected to see the entire sequence when visited by his two sons.

It had taken a good bit of persuading for Logan to talk his older brother into allowing him to ride along. He'd argued both of them should be there, asking questions and hearing answers. There was a good chance their father would refuse to talk about his actions.

Straightening, Quinn stretched out his knotted muscles, exhaling a slow breath. His gaze moved to Logan.

"It's been close to twenty years since he and your mother were together. We both know he was weak regarding her. He never intended to leave my mother, and ended the affair with yours. How long did he continue seeing you?"

"He never stopped. I didn't know when he'd come by until he showed up. Mom would tell me to wait for him outside. So, he did continue to call her to arrange days with me." He let out a bitter snort. "She'd always get dressed up, fix her hair and makeup, hoping he'd want to see her again. I think she must've loved him, Quinn."

"It's good to know he didn't shirk his responsibility to you."

"I wasn't allowed to call him or come to your house. He knew I'd done an online search and found where he lived. There were days I was so angry at my parents, I might've driven to your place. I was afraid he'd never visit if I defied him."

"Maybe. My guess is he'd let a little time go by, then call your mother and set something up. He's not a vindictive man." Quinn massaged the back of his neck, bending to pick up a tool before looking at Logan. "I'm wondering what we have to gain by confronting him. I doubt we'd learn much more than what we already know."

Logan shrugged one shoulder. "Why he cheated in the first place? Why he kept seeing my mother for close to five years?"

"You're right. I'm just not sure what that will accomplish. My parents are happy, have been for a long time. It won't be long until Pop can hire a foreman and retire."

"Or sell."

"That's a possibility."

Logan's eyes widened for a moment. "You don't want the ranch?"

"If that's what they want, I'll be glad to run it."

"With changes." Logan laughed.

Quinn smiled. "Of course."

They returned to repairing the last breaks in the fence, neither talking until Logan spoke. "You're not going to talk to him?"

Quinn stopped to stare at Logan, his green eyes narrowed, the tone of his voice hard and final. "Can't see any reason to bring up something that happened years ago."

He held up his hands, palms out. "All right. I just wanted to be sure. So, what's next?"

Aiden Winter lowered himself into a worn, red vinyl booth, exhausted and unsure where to go next. He'd been following David Nielsen. The fugitive's twin brother, Blake, had been right about him staying at a cousin's in South Dakota. Aiden had missed him by a day, and the cousin claimed to have no idea where he was headed.

"Coffee?" A waitress who looked as if she'd been working a few hours too many stood by the booth.

"Please. Also a burger, medium rare."

"Fries?"

"Sure." Reaching into a pocket, he pulled out a photo of David. "Do you recognize this man?"

Taking the photo from his hand, she took a long look before handing it back. "Sorry. I've never seen him."

"It was worth a shot."

"I'll get your order in and bring the coffee."

He'd followed David into Nebraska, stopping at gas stations, diners, and drive-throughs. About thirty percent of the people he spoke with recognized him. A pretty high rate compared to his previous searches.

"Here you are. Let me know if you want anything else."

"Thanks."

The burger smelled and looked good. Same with the fries. The coffee was better than expected. His stomach growled, though the expected pang of hunger didn't occur. Staring at the food, he pushed it away.

Aiden had a good idea where David was headed. If the fugitive continued on his current route, he'd be in Brilliance, and at the entrance to Whistle Rock Ranch in a few hours.

Why would he enter the place where his brother could identify him? The smart decision would be to travel south or east, getting as far away from the northwestern states as fast and far as possible. Maybe cross the border into Mexico.

Aiden's experience with those who jumped bail or escaped from jail indicated they weren't always the brightest people. A few were off the charts smart. A few barely functional. He didn't know where David appeared on the scale. His guess would be above average.

"Don't like the burger?"

With a sheepish expression, he glanced up at the waitress. "Guess my mind is on other stuff."

"Let me warm it for you. I know you aren't from around here, so you'll need something to get where you're going."

Aiden didn't argue when she picked up his plate and strolled toward the kitchen.

Blake spotted Abigail through the kitchen window while ratcheting up his courage. Deciding it wouldn't be the end of the world if she turned him down, he removed his hat before entering through the back door.

"Afternoon, Abbie."

"Hello, Blake. Is there something I can get for you?"

Fingering the edges of his hat, he stepped closer. "You probably know about the bounty hunter coming to the ranch."

A slight smile curved her lips. "I'm pretty sure everyone at the ranch knows about him."

"Yeah. Well, the man he wants is my twin brother."

"I heard that, too. Must be hard having your past thrust at you."

"Yeah, it is. It's something I have to deal with until my brother is found. Anyway, I came by to see if you'd want to ride with me to practice tonight."

The invitation surprised her. Quinn hadn't mentioned picking her up tonight. With his brother showing up, he might've even forgotten about it.

"That would be nice."

His eyes brightened, a boyish smile appearing. "Great. We'll leave here at six-thirty."

"I'll be ready." Reaching toward a plate, she picked up two cookies left from lunch. "Here. I know how much you like your sweets."

"You noticed?"

"Beth says it's part of our job to know what the ranch hands enjoy. The truth is, all but one or two love dessert."

He took the cookies from her outstretched hand. "You've pegged me right. I do love sweets. See you at six-thirty."

This would be the team's last practice before their first game tomorrow. She could've driven herself, but Blake's offer would give her a chance to get to know him better.

Finishing preparations for dinner, she removed her apron. Abigail wanted to take a short trail ride. Virgil had mentioned how the wildflowers were thicker than normal this year. They lasted a short time, and Abigail was determined to see them before they disappeared.

She didn't often ride by herself. Today, she wanted to be alone. Working from sunrise to sunset gave her little time to think, work through issues which weighed on her.

Cinching the saddle, she finished tacking up the mare, leading her outside. The weather was perfect. Warm with a slight breeze. Mounting, she reined the mare to the west.

"Where are you headed?" Virgil stood close by, his arms crossed.

"Thought I'd ride out to see the wildflowers. They're west, right?"

"Who's going with you?"

"I'm going alone."

"I don't think so." Turning, he motioned at Blake. "You'll ride with Blake. The fence line needs checking out that way."

"But..."

"No one, not even the ranch hands, ride out alone, Abbie."

Blake jogged up to them. "Yeah, boss?"

"Abbie needs someone to ride with her. Get your horse."

"Sure thing."

"Wait for him, Abbie. I have to place the order for supplies." Virgil didn't wait for a response.

She could ride off, leaving Blake behind, but that would be wrong in several ways. When Virgil gave an order, he expected it to be carried out. Not doing so could result in her not being allowed to ride one of the ranch horses.

"Are you ready, Abbie?"

"Yes."

"Where would you like to ride?"

"West, if that works for you. I want to see the wildflowers before they disappear."

"You're right about riding west. Let's go while we still have good light."

Quinn parked his truck near the Whistle Rock Ranch barn, figuring he'd find Abigail in the kitchen. Climbing out, he did a quick scan of the area.

Sam and another ranch hand trained one of the sought-after Paints in one corral, while two other men worked with what Quinn guessed to be a two-year-old quarter horse in another. Ready to turn toward the lodge, he paused, seeing two riders about a hundred yards away.

Narrowing his gaze, he felt a surge of anger mixed with dismay. Abigail rode beside a ranch hand he couldn't identify from this distance.

"You just missed her." Barrel stood next to Quinn, feet shoulder width apart, arms crossed. "She was determined to ride out to see the wildflowers. Virgil asked Blake Nielsen to ride along."

Blake. Quinn knew the man was attracted to Abbie. What he didn't know was how she felt about Nielsen.

Chapter Seventeen

Aiden continued west on interstate eighty, following a clear trail left by David Nielsen. The man stopped two to three times in each town, spending enough time for employees to notice him. Aiden had no trouble finding people who recognized him from the poster.

Strange. Then again, David was an odd personality. What man would implicate his twin in a felony to avoid his own capture? Why would he allow his twin to be found guilty and remanded to prison for a crime he committed? This seemed particularly heinous to Aiden.

He'd encountered little traffic in this part of Wyoming. The least populated of the continental states, its main industries were mineral extraction, tourism, and agriculture, including livestock. After stopping in Laramie and Cheyenne, he passed miles of open space. Aiden would have to make a decision soon on which highway to take north.

The bigger question in Aiden's mind centered on the reason David would head to Whistle Rock Ranch. The fugitive knew his brother worked there, which worried Aiden. Did he plan to do Blake harm? If so, he'd be facing much more than a few years in prison.

Telling himself to chill and enjoy the scenery, he relaxed his tense muscles. As the miles raced by, his mind moved to a time when he was fifteen, when the same image had been impressed on his brain.

His parents had taken a family vacation from their home in Montana. A road trip instead of flying to Hawaii or some other exotic location suggested by Aiden.

He and his older brother sat in the back seat of the family's silver sedan. They counted license plates, trying to tag all the states. Their odds to reach their goal lowered considerably when they crossed the border into Wyoming.

When bored with waiting for more vehicles to pass by them, the boys had begun a discussion of which state they'd want to live in after graduating from college. Rock, paper, scissors had determined Aiden would start first. As his brother, Ryan, expected, he chose Hawaii.

"If that's what you want, you should go to the University of Hawaii. You'll get to know locals and have a better chance of obtaining a job." Heading into his senior year at eighteen, Ryan had spoken as if he'd traveled the world. Aiden had always looked up to him.

"Maybe I will."

"You'll need a scholarship, Aiden," his mother had said from her spot in the passenger seat in front of them.

His features had fallen. "I know."

All four members of the Winters family had expected Ryan to receive numerous scholarship offers. At fifteen, Aiden remembered thinking he had time to make his mark in academics. Except, he had never done great in the classroom. A solid B student, he'd excelled at sports.

Football, baseball, and summer soccer league. He'd been a star in all three.

A car horn blasting brought him out of his mental ramblings. The timing couldn't have been better. Up ahead was the first turnoff north. The upcoming road, as well as the one a mile farther on, would get him to Brilliance and Whistle Rock Ranch.

Mentally flipping a coin, it came up heads for the first option. Aiden knew he'd be navigating a country road. Checking the fuel level, he pulled into the closest, and possibly only, gas station. It was one where customers were required to go inside to leave a credit card before pumping gas. This worked for him, as he planned to show David's picture to the employee inside.

His luck held. The clerk identified David within seconds of seeing the image.

"He was headed north. Mentioned the town where he was going, but I don't remember it."

"Could it have been Brilliance?"

The clerk snapped his fingers. "Yeah. That was it."

Filling the tank, Aiden considered how he'd approach David. The fugitive would find a nondescript motel for the night. Maybe the one Aiden stayed at during his last trip.

He'd been so close to capturing him in South Dakota at a cousin's house. One day separated the two, with David leaving the state less than twenty-four hours before Aiden arrived.

The bounty hunter had been deflated when presented with the evidence at Whistle Rock Ranch. Blake could prove he wasn't the man who'd gone to jail for committing a felony. His family and friends had backed him, giving his lawyer additional information to force his release.

Continuing his drive north, he reflected on something David's cousin in South Dakota said. She'd told him she hadn't seen David in some time, that the cousin who'd left was Blake. Aiden had responded by correcting her, but she'd insisted the man who stayed with her was Blake. He'd chuckled, realizing even family members couldn't tell them apart.

Well, it would be resolved soon. The moment he took David into custody.

Abigail realized she'd made a mistake within minutes of getting into Blake's truck. His entire demeanor changed when he drove away from the ranch.

"How about we forget practice and get dinner somewhere? You know, just the two of us." As he spoke, his hand had moved to her knee. She'd shoved it away, giving him a warning glance before scooting closer to her door.

"I don't think so. Tomorrow is our first game, and I want to be ready. Besides, I'm seeing Quinn."

Chuckling, he withdrew his hand, placing it on the steering wheel. "He's not good enough for you, Abbie. You'd be better off going out with me."

"I've known Quinn a while, and he's a great guy."

"So am I."

"I'm sure you are, Blake. And I do appreciate our friendship."

"It could be much more." He turned toward the community park, slowing his speed. "If you'd agree to a date, I could show you."

Checking her phone, she saw a message from Quinn. Opening it, she sighed. He'd gone by the ranch to pick her up.

She forced her voice to stay calm. "Not as long as I'm seeing Quinn. Can you please speed up a bit? It takes me a while to get into my catcher's gear."

His grin twisting into a snarl, he pressed the accelerator. Pulling into a parking spot, he slammed on the brakes, causing her to slide forward.

"Hey!"

"Sorry. Pushed too hard on the pedal."

Releasing a breath, she bit her tongue to avoid saying something she'd regret. "Thanks for the ride."

"I'll meet you here after practice for the drive to the pizza place."

"Let me think about it, Blake." Climbing out, she opened the back door to grab her gear bag.

"I'll carry that for you."

"Got it. Thanks again." Fuming all the way to the spot where the team slipped into their gear, she was glad to see Sam's infectious smile.

"You look as if someone stole your favorite shoes."

Forcing a weak chuckle, Abigail decided not to make an issue of Blake's attitude or driving. She dropped her bag to the ground. "Just a long day. Is everyone here?"

"All but Quinn. I thought you'd be riding with him."

"I know he's on his way. I'm hoping he can give me a ride to the pizza place."

"If not, I've got my truck. I wouldn't mind a few minutes of girl time."

Abigail pulled on her knee and shin pads. "How about you and I get together after work next week? I wouldn't mind some girl time myself."

"You let me know what works. Ah, there's Quinn."

Turning toward the parking area, Abigail watched Quinn and another man exit his truck. She assumed he was Quinn's brother, Logan.

"I texted you." Quinn's words caused her to wince.

"Sorry I didn't respond. There were, well...circumstances. I'll explain later." She faced the other man. "You must be Logan. I'm Abbie."

"Good to meet you, Abbie. So, you're the catcher."

A smile curved her lips as she looked down at the pads. "Seems so. Are you going to play?"

"Maybe. I played from the time I was six until graduating from high school."

"Then that will make you one of the most experienced players on the team. What position?"

Logan shrugged, his gaze moving across the group of people standing around. "Just about all of them. I was never a catcher, though."

"Hey, Sam." Abigail motioned her to join them. "This is Logan. He works with Quinn. Do we have room for him on the team?"

Sam held out her hand, gripping Logan's. "We could sure use a utility player. Would that work for you?"

"Perfect."

"Great. Come with me and I'll get you a glove."

When the two were far enough away not to hear, Abigail lowered her voice. "I hadn't heard from you. When Blake offered me a ride, I took it."

Quinn's lips twisted in a snarl. "Blake..."

"Well, it was a mistake." She glanced around until certain they were alone. "Something isn't quite right with him."

Brows scrunching, he placed a hand on her shoulder. "What did he do?"

She shook her head. "It's more what he said. Any chance I can ride to the pizza place with you and Logan?"

"I'm counting on it." Bending down, he kissed her cheek.

Quinn didn't stop at Whistle Rock Ranch, preferring to take Logan to the Kelman place before driving Abigail home. The pizza restaurant hadn't been private enough to discuss her comment about Blake Nielsen. They'd have plenty of time to talk at Whistle Rock.

Parking, he reached out, drawing her toward him. "That's better. Now, tell me what Blake did on your drive to the community park."

"It wasn't what he did, although his driving became erratic after he asked me out."

Quinn lifted a brow. "He asked you out?"

"Yes. There are men who find me attractive."

"I know. I'm one of them. What surprises me is he knows we're going out."

"Blake didn't act as if he cared. He appears to have a high opinion of himself. When I told him I was dating you, he became angry."

"That's when his driving became erratic." Quinn's lips drew into a tight line.

"Yes. The Blake I saw tonight was opposite of what everyone sees on the ranch. Almost as if he's two different people. It made me uncomfortable. I won't be riding with him again."

Kissing her, Quinn walked Abigail to the kitchen door, waiting until she walked inside. Considering what she'd told him and the actions which unnerved her tonight, his thoughts rested on a few words.

Almost as if he's two different people.

Chapter Eighteen

David Nielsen held his binoculars steady, watching Whistle Rock Ranch from inside his truck. He'd spent the night in the back seat, not wanting to spend money on a motel room. Nor did he desire his presence be known. Not until he sorted everything out.

His aunt had received a handful of texts from his brother. Each one provided more information about the ranch where he worked and some woman who'd caught his attention. The last was so like his twin. He'd always jumped from one woman to another, never staying with one for more than a few months.

When his aunt had received a phone call from someone looking for him, David knew it was time to move on. Less than an hour later, he hit the road for Wyoming.

Reaching below the seat, he pulled out a thermos of coffee his aunt had packed. Another bag held coffee cake and apples. The cooler was supplied with sliced meat, cheese, yogurt, and the small carrots his aunt fed her horse every so often.

Eating a slice of coffee cake with his coffee, he lifted the binoculars again. At seven in the morning, a group headed into the large lodge at seven, leaving their work until after breakfast.

An hour later, he adjusted the binoculars. His gaze swept the area near the barn, spotting his brother standing with a few other men near one of the corrals. The sight brought conflicting sensations. Love and anger contradicted each other, but he felt both when he watched his twin.

Finishing his breakfast, David thought through the best way to approach his brother. The most obvious would be to obtain the help of local law enforcement. This option would be risky. He remembered his aunt saying the sheriff had been brought in when a bounty hunter showed up looking for David. She showed him the emails from his brother. They were short, consistent with his brother's style of communicating.

"Don't move." Aiden aimed his gun at David.

David startled at the harsh voice behind him. He didn't attempt to look.

"Now raise your hands."

He didn't, choosing to turn toward the voice. "Who are you?"

"Aiden Winters."

"Ah. The bounty hunter."

Aiden didn't respond. Instead, he pulled the wanted poster from his pocket, handing it to David.

Reading it, he scoffed, handing it back. "Good luck with that."

Frowning, Aiden tucked it away. "Already have good luck. I found you, didn't I? Now, turn around." He pulled out a zip tie.

"Not going to happen. You want to shoot me? Go for it." Turning back toward the ranch, he lifted the binoculars.

Aiden watched for a minute, curious as to what David was doing. He could knock him out, use the zip tie and load him into his truck. Something about the man stopped him.

"Why your interest in Whistle Rock Ranch?"

David didn't answer for several seconds. "Watching my brother."

"The one you set up for your crime."

"You're wrong about that, but we'll discuss it later."

"How am I wrong?"

Sighing, he lowered the binoculars. "My aunt tells me he's doing real good. Interesting, as he never liked ranch work. Preferred to make money using his head, not his hands. Same with baseball. My aunt said he's on the ranch's team. An outfielder I believe."

"What's so odd about that?"

"He hated all sports except football. Didn't even watch other sports on TV. I was the one who played baseball. Third base."

Aiden moved to step beside him, his gaze sweeping over David for weapons. "What are you saying?"

"Just that the emails he sent our aunt talk about activities he's never enjoyed. Odd, don't you think?" Opening the door of his vehicle, David set the binoculars on the seat before turning to face Aiden. When the bounty hunter didn't respond, he shrugged. "I'm not who you're after."

Aiden choked out a piercing laugh. "Do you have any idea how often I hear that?"

"I don't really care. In this case, you're chasing the wrong man." He walked to within a foot of Aiden. Standing almost toe-to-toe, his voice hardened. "I'm not David Nielsen. I'm his twin, Blake."

Quinn motioned for Abigail to follow him on a narrow trail taking them into the forest. He'd talked her into a short ride before their first ball game that afternoon. Beth didn't object to her taking the time off, and he'd asked Logan to fill in for him.

"This is beautiful."

Quinn shot a look over his shoulder. "Wait until you see what's in the meadow ahead."

She thought of her ride with Blake, remembering how he'd acted strange, similar to how he'd been when he drove them to their practice. The change in demeanor had alarmed her, putting Abigail on alert. She still wrestled with saying something to Beth, knowing her boss would talk to Jake, who would pass along Abigail's concerns to Virgil.

Following his lead, she sucked in a breath when Quinn reined to a stop. Before them was a gorgeous meadow filled with spring wildflowers. Yellow agoseris, blue western monkshood, orange mountain dandelions, and red columbine covered the ground between them and where the forest closed around them.

"They're magnificent, Quinn."

"I thought you'd enjoy seeing them. They'll continue blooming for a couple months, but the color is the most vivid now."

Lifting her phone, she took several pictures. "If these turn out, I'm going to frame them for my apartment."

"Great idea. Are you ready for the game tonight?"

"Nervous, but ready. Beth and Jake are going to try to make it."

"So are Wyatt and Daisy."

Taking a few more pictures, she slid the phone away. "I think Lily is going to ride with them. Lily told Beth she wants to play, but her schedule at the hospital makes it difficult to be at the games."

Quinn chuckled. "I'm almost certain the team manager will let her play when she isn't working."

"Virgil doesn't want to show favoritism toward his wife."

"Come on, Abbie. Name one person on the team who would complain?"

Her mouth twisted as she thought, a grin forming. "No one."

"Right. Are you ready to see something else?"

"I am."

Reining his horse around, Abigail followed, glancing behind her at the colorful meadow. She'd ride out again, maybe with Beth.

Slowing his horse, Quinn rode beside Abigail for several minutes before clearing his throat to speak. "Have dinner with me on Sunday."

"I'd love to."

"Really?"

"Of course. Why wouldn't I?"

"The last time didn't work out as I planned."

"Quinn, I had a wonderful night. Humberto's was perfect. The food was as good, or better than most places in the area."

He chuckled. "For a woman who loves to cook, I forgot how easy you are to please."

"Easy when the food is good. Where do you plan to take me tomorrow?"

"Wherever you want to go, Abbie."

"Run, Abbie!" Quinn's voice cut through the evening air, encouraging her to pump her already burning legs faster. "Slide! Slide!"

Releasing a breath, she sent up a quick prayer before diving toward third base. Fingers slid across rubber an instant before her opponent received the ball, touching her with his mitt.

"Safe!"

Not immediately rising, she pulled her legs underneath her aching body, and knees shaking, stood. It was then she

150

heard applause and whoops. She'd hit a triple on her first at bat of the season.

"Great slide, Abbie." Virgil, acting as the third base coach, smiled. His face sobered when he saw her wince. "Are you all right?"

Voice flat, she nodded. "Great."

"You may want to put some ice on your right knee. It's turning purple."

Glancing down, her lips twisted in a wry grin. "Not until I score."

Virgil barked out a laugh as Quinn stepped to home plate. With an easy swing, he sent the ball over a short fence in right field.

Watching the ball fly through the air, Abigail started for home plate, surprised at the sharp pain in her knee. Stumbling, she stopped for an instant, fighting to stay upright. Resting for several beats of the clock, she sucked in a deep breath. At least forty steps to go.

"Want some help, Abbie?"

Startling at Quinn's voice, she gave a sharp nod. Abigail could be stubborn, but chose to protect her knee. "Sure."

Wrapping an arm around her waist, he provided assistance until a foot before the plate. "I'll catch you on the other side."

She gave another nod, touched home plate, then stopped to let Quinn catch up. "Nice hit."

"Nice home run," she returned as he helped her to the bench.

Abigail sat out the rest of the game, her place as catcher filled by Quinn's brother, Logan. She had to admit he did a real fine job.

The scoreboard showed Whistle Rock Ranch Wranglers winning by four runs when the game ended.

"Are you up for celebrating with pizza?" Quinn stood over her, his tired, satisfied smile reflected how he felt.

"I'm starving." Standing, she didn't hesitate to lean into him when his arm circled her waist.

"Great. Hey, Logan. Are you ready to go?"

"Sure am." Slinging his gear bag over one shoulder, he bent down to pick up Abigail's larger bag.

They entered the pizza parlor several minutes later, joining the others in one corner. Abigail couldn't miss the narrow gaze Blake shot her. The man who'd worn a smile since coming to the ranch had changed. And it wasn't for the better. She found herself wondering what had dampened the man's congenial attitude.

"Same pizza as always, Abbie?" Quinn helped her sit down at one of the long picnic tables inside the restaurant.

"Please." Relaxing, she stretched out her right leg. The relief lasted a few moments before she adjusted the position again.

Laughing at something Barrel said, her gaze switched to the man next to him. Blake still wore the strangled expression of a man attempting to hide his unease.

When he glanced up, his cold, gray eyes locked with hers. An icy chill washed over her, lodging in her chest.

Chapter Nineteen

Standing at one of the prep stations in the kitchen, Abigail bent down, adjusting the knee brace Virgil had given her. Thank goodness the injury wasn't serious. The pain had receded, as had the swelling, which made standing easier.

She'd tried to beg off dinner with Quinn that evening, not wanting her bum knee to ruin their time together. He'd responded by saying he had no problem carrying her if walking became too difficult. She'd laughed, grateful for his sense of humor.

"How are you feeling this morning?" Beth set down a small bag before removing a lightweight jacket.

"Better. Virgil gave me a brace. I should be fine for next Saturday's game."

"At least your slide into third base was awesome. Almost makes up for the pain."

Abigail nodded on a chuckle. "Yeah, almost. Thanks for posting about breakfast this morning being juice, coffee, fruit, and pastries. It was easy to set out."

"Thank you for being here with your bum knee. Jake and I had been wanting to attend church for a while. So, lunch." Beth walked to the posted menu. "Chicken salad sandwiches, roast beef sandwiches, fresh fruit, homemade potato chips, cookies, and lemon squares. I can handle that by myself. Dinner is one of their favorites. Oven fried chicken, red skinned potatoes, green beans, fresh baked bread, and pie for dessert. Both the bread and pies are frozen, so those are easy."

"The chicken is prepared and ready to bake. They're on trays in the refrigerator. Same with the potatoes and green beans. Those are in sealed bags."

Beth opened one of the large refrigerators, seeing the food. "You have been busy this morning."

"There's a reason, Beth. Quinn asked me to dinner tonight. I need to be ready by six-thirty. I'll be here to help cook the food and serve dinner."

"Fine with me. Cleaning up will be easy. Do you know where you're going?"

"Quinn hasn't said."

Beth opened her mouth to respond, closing it at the sound of men shouting from outside. The women rushed to the window to see a group of men circling Virgil, Wyatt, and two other men.

"Can you see the two men with Wyatt and Virgil?"

Abigail moved from the window to the door, stepping outside for a better view. Focusing on those in the center of the group, her breath caught.

"It looks like, well..." She took several paces forward. Pressing her lips together, she blinked a few times. "I believe Virgil and Wyatt are talking to Blake and another man who looks just like him." She looked at Beth. "It must be his twin."

Wyatt's gaze switched between David, the twin who insisted he was Blake, not David, and Aiden Winters. He shot a glance at Virgil, who shrugged in confusion.

Wyatt turned to face Aiden. "Have you spoken to Sheriff Dugan?"

"Not yet, but I'll be seeing him soon." Aiden thought of the ankle monitor he'd attached around David's ankle. The man couldn't get more than one hundred and fifty feet from Aiden without the bounty hunter knowing. He wished one could be placed around Blake's ankle, the same as he wanted there to be a definitive way to tell them apart.

Aiden had done considerable research on twins. He'd also studied the notebook Blake said he prepared, which exonerated him. His job now was to use what he had to make a determination on which of the men standing next to him was the escaped fugitive, David Nielsen. His instincts told him it was the man working at Whistle Rock Ranch.

Aiden knew DNA couldn't be used to make a firm determination between identical twins. There were subtle ways to tell one twin from another, however, that was what Aiden planned to do.

Using the notebook containing pictures and news clipping, plus the information gleaned from a phone call with the aunt, Aiden knew the real David had a birthmark on his neck, while Blake had one on his chest. David also had a mole on his cheek.

The twin Aiden had tracked from South Dakota, the one he thought was the guilty one, didn't have a visible mole or birthmark.

Moving fast, surprising everyone, Aiden grabbed David's arm, twisting it behind the man's back. He was the man everyone on the ranch called Blake.

"Don't do anything foolish," Aiden growled into the fugitive's ear before zip tying the man's wrists together and leading him away.

Quinn took Abigail's hand in his, squeezing with a light touch. They sat next to each other in a fifties style diner with red vinyl bench seats. The floor was checkered with black and white vinyl tiles, and the white walls covered with pictures of pop stars of the fifties.

Neither had been to the Jackson, Wyoming, restaurant since its opening a few weeks earlier. The menu continued the color scheme and offered burgers, fries, chili, shakes, malts, and various flavors of cola. Vanilla had a star next to it, indicating it was a favorite.

"Good evening. I'm Tina. What would you like to drink?"

Both glanced up to see a twenty-something waitress wearing black shorts, a white blouse, tennis shoes, and cute red cap.

"A regular cola for both of us," Quinn said.

"All right. I'll be back in a second to take your food order."

"Perky," Abigail said a few seconds after the efficient waitress left.

"Yeah." Quinn squeezed her hand while tapping fingers on the tabletop with his other hand. "Blake, or I should say David, sure fooled a lot of people."

This was the first either of them had brought up the strange occurrence at the ranch earlier that day. Quinn hadn't been there, hearing the account from both Abigail and Beth.

"He sure did, including me."

"You said Aiden took David away. Did the real Blake leave with them?"

She shook her head. "No. Virgil and Wyatt wanted to talk to him. The last I saw, they were going into the lodge with Jake."

"Probably to offer him a job."

"That's my guess. The entire situation between the twins is sad. I can't imagine what their family life must have been like to turn out two brothers so different."

Quinn rested an arm around Abigail's shoulders. "It's real fortunate Aiden figured it out."

Seeing movement from the corner of his eye, he spotted the waitress approaching, removing his arm.

"Have you decided what you want?"

When she walked away a few minutes later, Quinn's attention moved to Abigail. "I'm glad you were able to get the evening off."

"Me, too. Beth's flexible. I try not to take advantage."

They ate and talked about various topics over the next hour. Abigail mentioned the puppies someone had dropped off at the ranch, including their return to the owner.

"It was harder than I expected."

Quinn ate the last of his fries, using his drink to swallow. "You grew attached to them."

"One in particular. I even picked out a name."

"What was it?"

She grinned over the rim of her glass. "Rowdy."

"Great name. What made you select it?"

"The puppy I picked out was boisterous and tough. He refused to be pushed around by the bigger puppies. He also loved to be held."

"Affectionate?"

"Very. It was silly of me to get so attached to him."

"I don't believe it was silly, Abbie." He ran a finger down her cheek. "The puppy caught your interest. There was a connection. You didn't know the real owner would show up."

"I'm the one who took them to Doc Worrel's office. She had an idea who they belonged to. I should've forgotten about him."

"Do you know if the owner sold the puppies?"

"It's been a few weeks. I assume he did."

Quinn was going to ask if she'd thought about calling the owner to see if Rowdy was still available. His thoughts were interrupted when his phone rang.

"Yeah, Jake."

Abigail finished her burger, sipping her drink while Quinn talked to her brother. She found herself wondering where the relationship was going. They'd done the dating thing in Sheridan before Quinn left for the job in Idaho.

Those months had been a special time for both of them. Friends told her they were meant for each other. Abigail had never been so happy, convincing herself they might have a future together.

She'd been angry when he'd left without talking to her in person. Instead of answering any of the many messages he'd left, her pride took over. It had been immature not to answer any of them.

"Are you sure, Jake? Okay. I'll be back in a bit. Call if you need help." He slid the phone away, staying quiet for a minute before looking at Abigail.

"The bull and cows have arrived."

"Tonight?"

"They were to arrive earlier today. I got a call saying they'd be delivered tomorrow. Guess they decided to go forward without notifying me."

"Do you want to head home?"

"When we're finished. Jake is there. So is Logan and most of the ranch hands." Grabbing the glass filled with water, he drank what remained.

Knowing Quinn was anxious to get back, Abigail waved to the waitress.

"Thank you for a wonderful evening, Abbie." Quinn walked her to the back door, stopping on the low stoop. "I know we have a game on Saturday, but I want to see you again, as soon as Beth will give you another evening off."

"Tell me when and I'll make it work."

A slight grin curved the corners of his mouth upward. "This coming Wednesday."

"I'm sure it will be all right with Beth."

"Good." Resting his hands on her shoulders, he pressed his lips to hers before wrapping his arms around her. Deepening the kiss, he finally pulled back on a sigh.

"Ah, Abbie." He rested his forehead against hers. "I'd better get going. I'll pick you up for Saturday's game at six." He stayed long enough to confirm she was inside before returning to his truck.

Looking out the window, Abigail watched him drive away, her heart beating a staccato rhythm. Waiting until her breathing slowed, she walked to the bulletin board to check the menu for the following day. Nothing that would benefit being started tonight.

Walking through the kitchen, she headed straight for her apartment. Though she had keys, Abigail never locked the door.

Closing the door behind her, she froze. An unfamiliar sound came from her bedroom. A rustling noise and what she believed to be a whimper.

Setting her jacket down, she took careful steps through the living room, past the kitchen, then stopped. The sounds came again.

Curiosity had her feet moving forward. Reaching the door to her bedroom, she inched it open. Her jaw dropped at what she saw on the floor.

Rushing forward, she knelt beside a lined bed. Inside, eyes wide and staring up at her was a puppy. Not just any puppy, but a very special one.

Around his neck was a purple ribbon. She read the gold lettering.

Rowdy.

Chapter Twenty

A soft, strangled bark, followed by several more, awakened Abigail. Blinking, she rolled toward the bed stand. Five o'clock. She'd slept about four hours. When the bark came again, she sat up, then jumped out of bed.

She dropped to the floor, making cooing sounds while lifting Rowdy to her chest. "You are just the cutest puppy I've ever seen."

Setting him in front of the food and water dishes. Rowdy focused on the food as if he hadn't eaten in days. Abigail dressed while the puppy ate, gently shoving him away when he went after her shoelaces.

Picking Rowdy up, she grabbed his bed with her other hand before heading for the kitchen. Beth stood at the counter, preparing the standard breakfast. Abigail stopped close to her.

"Is this your doing?" She held up Rowdy and his bed.

Beth ran a hand over the puppy's head and back. "Only a tiny part."

"Really?" She set Rowdy and the bed on the floor. "Who else?"

A grin played at the corners of Beth's mouth. "Quinn."

Abigail's eyes flashed. "What? But how did he know about Rowdy? I just told him last night."

"Jake mentioned the puppies. Quinn asked me about them. The rest was his doing. He called Doc Worrel for the name of the breeder and found out he'd only sold one of the puppies. The litter was all female except for one."

"Rowdy..." Abigail whispered.

"Quinn called Jake a few minutes before bringing you home last night. Your brother brought Rowdy, the bed, and food over here. Stayed until you got here." Beth laughed. "You missed him by minutes."

Abigail stared down at Rowdy, who busied himself chewing at her shoelaces. "I assumed you bought him."

"I thought about it, but you said a puppy would be too much work. Quinn decided to go for it anyway. Probably thought he would keep Rowdy if you didn't want him."

Kneeling down, Abigail picked up the puppy, snuggling him against her. "As if I wouldn't keep you."

"I'd better finish. The ranch hands will be showing up within thirty minutes."

"Let me find a place for Rowdy so I can help."

"Quinn left a pet playpen for you to use. It's leaning against the wall over there." Beth nodded toward the freezer.

"Wow. He thought of everything."

Carrying Rowdy, she set him down long enough to open and place the playpen where she wanted it. Putting the puppy inside, she added the bed.

"It even has a door."

"That's what Quinn said. He was surprised to find it in Brilliance."

"Well, he did a fine job." Brows furrowed, Abigail noticed Rowdy hadn't moved from where she placed him. He cocked his head to the side, panting, as his huge brown eyes stared at her. Her heart melted at the expectant look on the puppy's face.

Beth glanced over her shoulder. "He's already got you wrapped around his tiny paw."

"I'm afraid you're right. But we have work to do." She washed her hands, slipped on an apron, and began cooking pancakes as voices came from the dining room.

"The ranch hands have arrived." Beth smiled, scooping eggs into a covered serving dish.

Abigail thought of calling Quinn to thank him for Rowdy, deciding to wait until he picked her up for the game that evening. She was excited and a little nervous about facing this opponent.

Beth, Jake, and most of the people from both ranches would be in the stands to cheer them on. From what she'd heard, a good number of townsfolk loved attending the games. With the snow gone, the temperatures up, and the ground no longer muddy, the crowd should be pretty good.

A trip to town resulted in a large bag of toys and treats for Rowdy. Abigail spent the time between meals playing with the way too cute puppy.

Several of the ranch hands had heard about Rowdy, and stopped by to see him. Rowdy was so overwhelmed by their attention, he finally curled into a ball of exhaustion and slept.

It didn't take long for Abigail to feel the same fatigue. A quick glance at the clock indicated she had time for a nap before prepping for dinner.

"You should talk with the women, Jonah. What do I know about gift baskets?" Gage Bonner headed straight to the refrigerator to grab a snack. "Do you want something?"

His older brother looked over Gage's shoulder. "Hand me one of those energy drinks."

Taking what they wanted, Gage closed the refrigerator door. That's when the brothers noticed Abigail.

"Hey, Abbie. Heard you got a puppy." Gage looked around her to the pet playpen. "What's his name?"

"Rowdy."

"The little guy looks all tuckered out." Jonah stepped past Gage to peer down at the puppy. "Judging by the size of his paws, he'll grow to around sixty pounds. His color will probably darken with age."

Smiling, she thought of the difference between the three Bonner brothers. Wyatt, the oldest, was married to Daisy and loved ranching. Gage, the youngest brother, spent most of his time outdoors. Tan and muscled, he couldn't get enough of various extreme sports.

The middle brother, Jonah, was the quietest of the three. With MBA and law degrees, he handled the finances and did the initial research on all potential business deals for the ranch. The most analytical of the three, he'd be the one to make comments about Rowdy's size and color.

"He was a gift." She leaned into the playpen when Rowdy woke up. Picking him up, she handed the puppy to Jonah.

Looking at the ribbon, he smiled. "Rowdy. At least we know what to expect."

Gage stepped close, fluffing the puppy's fur. "You should ask Abigail about gift baskets."

"Good idea." Jonah handed Rowdy to Gage. "A woman contacted me about moving her business to Brilliance. She sells gift baskets and other items. Her attorney did some research and learned we have an industrial building. It isn't for lease, though I'd consider it if the numbers make sense. Do you know anything about the gift basket business?"

"Only that I've bought them. Usually online since little is available in Brilliance."

"I see. Do you know if they're popular?"

"Very. You can send almost anything using gift baskets. Themed baskets are common. Desserts, cheese and meats, reading items, gifts for newborns, puppy and dog items. The kinds of baskets are endless. Are you able to obtain her sales information?"

"We'll request financial statements if the decision is to consider leasing the building."

"I believe there's a shop that carries gift baskets in Jackson. It might be worth a trip."

"Good idea, Abbie. Thanks."

Gage held Rowdy out toward Abigail. "I need to get going. Let me know if you ever need someone to watch over your puppy."

"Thanks. I appreciate the offer." She held Rowdy in the crook of her arm. "Do you want me to make sandwiches to take with you?"

Jonah shook his head. "It's not long until dinner. We plan to be at your game tonight to cheer the team on."

"So you better win." Gage grinned, holding the back door open for his brother.

Abigail couldn't stop the nervous energy coursing through her as she dressed for the game. She checked the time. Quinn, along with Logan, would be arriving soon to pick her up.

Picking up her equipment bag, Abigail checked on a sleeping Rowdy before heading outside. She spotted Quinn's truck right away. Taking the bag from her, he set it in the back before opening the passenger door. Before she climbed inside, Abigail faced him.

"Thank you so much for Rowdy. It was a complete surprise." Getting on her toes, she kissed his cheek.

"My pleasure, Abbie. I'm guessing you plan to keep him." The corner of his eyes crinkled with humor.

She chuckled. "You know very well I wouldn't consider sending him back."

Ten minutes later, they removed their gear from the bed of the truck. The game scheduled before theirs was in the bottom of the ninth inning. Perfect timing.

Setting her bag down, her attention shifted to a tall man walking toward the dugout. Narrowing her gaze, she was surprised to see Blake Nielsen. She hoped it was the real Blake. As he got closer, it occurred to her they'd never met.

"Hi. I'm Blake. You work in the kitchen, right?"

"Yes. I'm Abbie. It's good to meet you. Everyone is glad everything was sorted out."

"Thanks. Aiden Winters was the one to figure it out. Samantha told me my brother played on the team."

"Yes. He was an outfielder. I believe Logan is taking his place, but I'm pretty sure we need a utility player. Let's go check with Sam. She seems to know everything going on."

They spoke to Sam. As Abigail suspected, the team did need a utility player. Sam found a glove for Blake and introduced him to those players he didn't know.

Their game started right on time. The flip of a coin made the Whistle Rock Ranch Wranglers the home team. The lead changed each inning until the fourth when Barrel hit a screaming home run with two people on base.

The spectators whooped and clapped as Barrel ran the bases. They were still cheering when the next player came up to the plate.

Quinn watched as two balls sailed over the plate for strikes. The third pitch was low, just what he'd been hoping to get. He hit it hard to left field, watching as it flew over the fence for another home run.

The fans stood, yelling their approval or booing, depending on what side they were on. This put the Wranglers up by four runs.

The opposing team decided on a pitching change, giving Abigail a little more time to warm up. She'd never been a strong hitter. Her strength was speed. If she could get on base, the odds were excellent she'd steal second and third.

"You're up, Abbie," Sam called.

She'd paid no attention to the new pitcher until finalizing her stance in the batter's box. Positioning the bat, she locked gazes with Doctor Mason Nagle.

Chapter Twenty-One

Doctor Mason Nagle, one of the pitchers for the hospital's team, began his wind up. He loved baseball, had played it until being accepted into medical school. There'd been a point in his life when he thought about trying to make it with one of the professional organizations. His desire to be a doctor had won out.

It felt good to be doing something besides stitching up his emergency room patients. Being outside with people he worked with cleansed his mind, calming in a way nothing else ever had.

He'd arrived late, parking just minutes before the team manager, a husky nurse from cardiology, asked him to pitch. Mason knew they were playing the team from Whistle Rock Ranch, and they were expected to do well. He hadn't considered Abigail Kelman would be playing until his gaze locked on her intense caramel brown eyes.

Stopping his wind up, he straightened, forcing himself to relax. Mason had thought about her often since blowing her off for a date with another woman. He'd regretted his bad decision ever since.

Shrugging off their brief past, he began again, delivering a pitch way outside the strike zone. Concentrating, the next two pitches were strikes. One pitch away from sending Abigail back to the bench.

His next pitch traveled straight and true...right into Abigail's sweet spot. Her bat connected, sending the ball down the right field line. It rolled into the corner, allowing her to reach second base.

Her wide, bright smile punched Mason in the gut. Some decisions in life just don't allow a do-over.

Abigail packed her gear after an exhilarating eight to five victory over the hospital's team. She'd faced Mason three more times before the game ended. The tension at seeing him had disappeared. He'd become nothing more than the pitcher for the opposing team.

"Are you up for celebrating our win with ice cream?" Quinn's warm breath caressed her neck.

"I'd love ice cream. Let me text Monica. She offered to check on Rowdy."

"Let her know we won't be out much longer."

"Are you two ready?" Logan slung his gear bag over his shoulder. "I mentioned it to Blake."

Lifting her bag, Abigail headed toward the truck. "Good. I hope he joins us."

"Jake says he's doing real good at the ranch," Quinn said. "Blake has a lot more experience than his brother. He should be a real good hire for them."

"Abbie. Wait up." The three turned at the shout to see Mason jog toward them.

"Come on, Logan. We'll wait for Abbie in the truck."
Quinn bent down to her ear. "Be nice." Straightening, he
greeted Mason. "Good game, Doc. See you next time."

Mason gave a terse nod before stopping next to Abigail.
"Hey."

"Hey. Nice pitching."

"Not good enough. Your team has a lot of talent."

"Thanks. I recalled you told me you pitched in high
school."

"And college, but not while I was in medical school.
Feels good to play again."

She nodded, not knowing what else to say.

"I'm sorry about what happened, Abbie. What I did was
wrong, and not at all fair to you. Maybe someday you'll be
able to forgive me."

She held up a hand. "I've already forgiven you, Mason.
You know, all you had to do was tell me you'd met someone
else. I would've understood. And the truth is, we weren't
really involved. Going out a few times doesn't make a
relationship."

"It did make for a friendship, though. I'm sorry my
actions destroyed it."

Crossing her arms, she gave a bleak nod. "Maybe
someday..."

"I hope so." Mason stood there for a moment before
walking toward his car.

Abigail felt a wave of sadness wash through her. She
had liked Mason, enjoyed their time together. Maybe they'd
now be able to salvage their friendship.

While Rowdy scampered around her apartment, Abigail spent the time between preparing Sunday breakfast and lunch sending emails to her parents and friends.

Each one contained a picture of Rowdy and a brief explanation of how he'd come into her life. She didn't mention Quinn, not interested in what she knew would be stinging responses from her family.

Knowing Quinn had a presence on one particular social media network, she typed in the internet address. She also had an account, posting infrequently.

Searching for Quinn's page, she smiled at a picture of him standing outside a corral holding a bull. Abigail thought it might be the new animal delivered the previous week. Scrolling through other pictures, she paused on several from the game the previous evening.

One showed her crouched in the familiar catcher's stance, mitt up, waiting for the pitch. Another showed Quinn and Abigail talking on the sideline. Scrolling down, she saw an image of Quinn with his arm around Sam. It had been posted the first week of practice. She had to admit it was a great picture.

A knock on her door had her closing the laptop. Picking up Rowdy, she opened the door to find Beth standing in the hall. Abigail glanced at her phone.

"Gosh. Time got away from me. I'll be right out to help with lunch."

"Take your time. I've already set most of it out. You know how Sundays are."

Abigail did know. Since most of the ranch hands had the day off, they tended to saunter in anywhere between eleven in the morning and one in the afternoon. Some grabbed sandwiches and left, while others filled plates, relaxing in the dining room as they ate.

"Let me get Rowdy situated and I'll be out to help you, Beth."

Slipping into jeans, a blouse, and comfortable work shoes, she carried the playpen to the kitchen, setting Rowdy inside with water and food. Ready to join Beth, she whirled around at the sound of the back door opening.

"Quinn. What a wonderful surprise. I wasn't expecting you for lunch." A few seconds followed before Jake and Logan stepped inside.

"I invited them." Beth walked to Jake, kissing his cheek. "Lunch is set out in the dining room if you boys want to get started."

"I'm starving." Jake glanced at his companions. "Let's get in there before there's nothing left."

"We should join them, Abbie." Beth removed her apron.

Setting Rowdy back into his pen, she followed Beth into the dining room. Quinn had already filled his plate. His gaze settled on hers.

"There's an empty seat next to me, Abbie."

Her smile squeezed his chest. "Save it for me."

Selecting a sandwich, salad, and a handful of corn chips, she took the seat beside him. He hadn't started eating.

"You didn't have to wait for me."

"I wanted to." Picking up half a sandwich, he took a huge bite. She did the same. "How's Rowdy doing?"

"Great. He's so friendly and active."

"The name fits him. I don't think he's going to get real big. Doc Worrel told me he's a mini Bernedoodle. It's a cross between a Bernese Mountain dog and a poodle."

"I've never heard of it."

He picked up his second sandwich. "Neither had I. The doc said minis grow to between twenty-five and fifty pounds. There are a few living on local ranches, though they aren't considered a ranch dog. My experience is a lot of dogs can be trained to work on a ranch, so I wouldn't worry about that." Taking a bite, he chewed, washing it down with bottled water.

"Good to know, but I hadn't thought that far ahead."

"Listen up." Wyatt had entered from the kitchen, snatched a sandwich off the table, and stopped between the tables. "There's a bluegrass festival in Brilliance. Starts at five. Daisy and I are going. So are Virgil and Lily, plus several of the ranch hands. Pile in your trucks and join us. Did I mention it was free?"

Claps and woohoos followed.

"Count us in," Jake shouted.

Quinn smiled. "Same with me and Abbie."

Beth stood. "Guess its cold cuts, salad, and whatever's in the refrigerator for those who stay behind. I'll need your help getting everything ready, Abbie."

"I'll pass the word around." Virgil shoved away from his spot against one of the pine columns.

Abigail moved to stand, stopping when Quinn placed a hand on her arm. "Will you ride with me?"

She returned a grin, which clutched his chest. "I'd like that."

He watched her disappear into the kitchen before finishing his lunch. There were things they needed to discuss. Perhaps tonight would be the right time and place.

Chapter Twenty-Two

Abigail leaned toward Quinn. "They're very good." She clapped along with everyone else to the upbeat rhythm from the band on the stage. Four musicians, three men and a woman, and each could sing.

"They are," Quinn agreed, clapping with her. "The next group is the headliner."

Almost everyone from the ranch, plus a few men from Jake Kelman's spread, made up their large group. Though no one sat, blankets had been spread out and were dotted with several chairs. Beth had loaded two coolers with drinks, cold cuts, salad, and desserts. The same food those who stayed at the ranch would be eating for dinner.

"Hey, Blake. Good to see you." Quinn shook hands with Blake Nielsen. He'd been doing well, especially when taking into account his twin brother's arrest. "Any word on David?"

Shoving hands in his pockets, Blake's gaze shot to the stage before returning to Quinn. "He's back in jail. Aiden Winters sent me a note saying it would be quite a while before he's eligible for parole."

"Better him than you. Have you eaten?"

"No. Thought I'd get a hamburger or something."

Quinn shook his head. "No need. Beth packed plenty of food in the coolers. Check them out and take what you want. There are drinks, too."

"Thanks, Quinn." Nodding at Abigail, Blake headed straight for the food.

Ninety minutes later, the group packed up their belongings and loaded everything into their vehicles. With such early days, Quinn guessed they'd all be asleep within thirty minutes of arriving at the ranch.

Waiting until the others had driven away, he grabbed Abigail's hand. "How about a short walk before driving back?"

"Sounds perfect."

Silence enveloped them as they made a circle around the park. The band packed up their gear, talking in hushed tones to each other. A couple Chamber of Commerce employees bustled about, helping with whatever needed to be done before heading home. The mayor and two council members created their own small group, the mayor speaking animatedly, her hands moving with her words. Quinn wondered what had her so worked up.

"How are you and Logan doing?"

"We're doing fine. He works hard and wants to learn." Quinn stared up at a clear sky dotted with millions of stars. "It's just hard to accept I have a younger brother."

"Do you plan to say anything to your father?"

"We still haven't decided. We're both concerned about my mother finding out."

"Have you considered she may already know about Logan and his mother?"

Quinn's grip on Abigail's hand tightened, his mouth twisting into a hard line. "No."

"Women are often more insightful than many men believe. What about your sister?"

His brows drew together. "What about her?"

Quinn thought of his younger sister. Darlene had always been fragile, unable to handle disappointment.

"Assuming she doesn't know about Logan, how will she handle the news?"

"You've met her, Abbie. If she already knows of the affair, she would've said something to me. Darlene is unable to keep secrets, and would've been upset to learn of Logan. As far as my mother, you're right. She may already know."

"It's something to consider when you and Logan make a decision about speaking with Wallace."

Quinn hadn't planned to spend their time together talking about his father. Thinking of what he'd done left a sour taste in his mouth.

"Are you ready to leave for the ranch?"

Looking down at her, he drew her closer. "Almost."

Lowering his head, he pressed his mouth against hers. Quinn lingered, not wanting to break the contact until they were both out of breath. Lifting his head, he rested his forehead against hers.

"We should probably head back," he whispered against her lips.

"I suppose," she answered with little enthusiasm.

Chuckling, Quinn threaded his fingers through hers as they walked to his truck.

Abigail stood at home plate, gripping the bat with both hands as she assessed the opposing pitcher. Her attention focused on the tall, lanky cowboy from a neighboring ranch, who had been flawless so far.

This was the first time her team had faced the very talented group of players who were in first place. Whistle Rock Ranch stood in third, with six games left to play.

They were up against a deadline. In three weeks, the first group of vacationers would descend on the ranch. Their arrival could end the team's Saturday night games.

"You've got this, Abbie!"

"Hit it out of the park!"

The yells of encouragement continued from her dugout, the support warmed her. Taking a slow, deep breath, she exhaled, as ready as she'd ever be.

The first pitch burst past her. She hadn't even seen it.

Adjusting her grip, she refocused as the pitcher wound up for his second pitch. This one was wide. The third ripped across the plate for another strike. Determined not to be another of the batters the pitcher struck out, she settled into a relaxed stance, bat in the air.

The next pitch flew toward her. Blocking everything out, she concentrated on the ball. Her bat connected, sending a ground ball through the opening between their second baseman and short stop. Legs pumping, she hit first base an instant before the ball fell into the glove of their first baseman.

Her team did their best, but by the end of the game, the score showed Whistle Rock six, the other team ten.

"How about we go for burgers at the diner?" Quinn draped an arm over Abigail's shoulders, his voice carrying to their entire team.

Agreeing, the group converged at the longtime favorite of locals and vacationers. Chowing down on the best burgers and fries in town, with Abigail beside him, Quinn couldn't shake the feeling he'd come home.

"I was ready for a change from pizza. This was a wonderful idea, Quinn." Abigail bit down on another bite of her cheeseburger, groaning at the taste. "There's always much more than I could ever eat."

"I'll take care of whatever you leave behind." Leaning back in the booth, he popped another fry into his mouth. "I haven't been around Barrel much, but whenever I am, people are smiling."

"I know. He has a way with people. The guests love him."

"Jake says the ranch would be worse off if he ever left."

"Speaking of my brother, has he said anything to you about leaving Whistle Rock?" Abigail picked up her milkshake.

"Nothing. Why? Has Beth said something?"

"A few comments once in a while, but nothing straight out. I thought he might have mentioned leaving to you."

"I've gotten the impression Jake's going to stay here a few years before managing his own ranch." Quinn set down his drink. "Plans can change, though."

"He has a sweet deal with you as the foreman."

His gaze narrowed on Abigail. "Jake told you that?"

"No, but it's obvious. The fact you're running my brother's ranch says it all." Finishing her shake, she set the empty cup down. "Do you think you'll be staying long?"

Quinn thought about it for a minute before answering. "Eventually, I plan to buy my own place. I'll stay until then."

Abigail fidgeted with her napkin, tearing off little pieces of paper. "I see. Where do you think you'll buy a place?"

"It depends."

"On what?"

Reaching over, he took her hand in his. "On where we want to live."

It took her a moment for his words to register. "We?"

"Well, yes. What did you think? That I'd buy a place and not take you with me?"

Her jaw dropped before she slammed it shut. Not sure what to say, she licked her lips, sputtering for a few seconds before the words came to her.

"Is that a proposal, Quinn Sawyer?"

He rubbed the back of his neck. "Well, I suppose it is."

Brows lifting, she crossed her arms. "You suppose?"

Standing, he held out his hand. "Everyone else has headed back to the ranch. Come on. Let's get out of here."

Hesitating for an instant, she took his hand. "Where to?"

"There's a trio at the steakhouse I'd like to hear." He stepped outside, tightening his grip on her hand.

Digging in her heels, she stared at him. "A trio? You just asked me to marry you and you want to listen to music?"

"Technically, I haven't asked you yet. It was more of a suggestion." Opening the passenger door, he motioned her to climb inside. When she didn't move, he tilted his head to the side. "We could walk."

Dropping her head to look at the ground, she gave a slow shake. "All right. Let's walk."

"Great idea." Taking her hand again, he took the sidewalk south to the steakhouse.

Saturday night and the place pulsed with energy. Most of the dinner crowd had already eaten and left. Many of those left tapped their boots to the upbeat music.

Finding a table far enough away from the speakers so they could talk, Quinn ordered coffee and Abigail a cup of hot tea.

"Would either of you like pie? We still have a few pieces." Each shook their head at the short, slender waitress. "All right. I'll get coffee and tea right out to you."

"What do you think of the trio, Abbie?"

Relaxing in the chair, she worked to control her thundering heartbeat, and her voice. "They're very good. Have you heard them before?"

"Once. I came with Jake and Beth."

"Here you are." The waitress smiled as she set down their drinks, individual mini pitchers of cream, and a sugar caddy. "Let me know if you want anything else."

Thanking her, both added cream to their hot drinks. Gripping her cup with both hands, Abbie used it to steady her shaky hands.

When the guitarist announced they were taking a break, Quinn scooted his chair closer to Abbie. Reaching over, he peeled one hand off her cup. Keeping his voice even, he spoke the words he'd been waiting a long time to ask.

"I love you, Abbie. I can't imagine a life without you in it. Would you do me the honor of marrying me?"

Chapter Twenty-Three

Abigail's throat constricted at his question. She'd prayed a long time to have Quinn back in her life, making his proposal seem as if she were in a dream. The sincerity in his gaze told her heart what it needed to know. Covering their joined hands, she smiled as a tear rolled down one cheek.

"I love you so much, Quinn. I'd be honored to be your wife."

Slipping a box out of his pocket, he opened it to reveal a platinum ring with a stunning princess cut solitaire diamond. His eyes misting, he slipped it on her left ring finger. Wrapping his arms around her, he covered her mouth with his for a quick, searing kiss.

Hearing the musicians return, he lifted his head. "We have a lot to discuss."

She held her hand out to admire the ring. "It's so gorgeous."

"There were a lot of choices. I was a little nervous you wouldn't like it."

"It's perfect, Quinn."

He repeated his comment. "There is a lot to talk about."

"I know. Do you want to start tonight?"

"No better time, sweetheart." He ran a hand over her hair.

The waitress stopped by their table with a new pot of hot water and a teabag in one hand. In the other, she held a coffee carafe. "Would you like more to drink?"

"Please," Quinn answered. "And two pieces of warm peach pie with ice cream."

"Changed your minds, huh?" She smiled. "I'll be right back."

He stroked his knuckles down her cheek. "What do you want to talk about first?"

"Have you thought about our jobs? We both need to work."

"I don't see any reason to quit until purchasing a ranch. Jake is building a foreman's cabin near the main house. It'll be ready in a few weeks. We can live there."

"Beth told me he was building you a place. Will it be big enough?"

A grin lifted the corners of his mouth. "Jake talked to me about what we'd need."

"My brother knew?"

"He guessed. The cabin will have one bedroom, a bathroom, kitchen, laundry area, living room, and dining room. It should be fine for the two of us."

"Sounds wonderful."

Neither spoke as the waitress set down their slices of pie. Taking bites, each hummed at the wonderful mix of flavors. Setting down his fork, Quinn once again took her hand.

"My question is, how soon can we marry?"

Beth shrieked when she spotted the ring on Abigail's finger. "Is that what I think it is?"

Abigail felt her face heat. "If you think it's an engagement ring, then yes." She held the ring out for Beth to see. "Quinn asked me to marry him last night."

Opening her arms, Beth hugged her. "I'm so excited for the two of you." Stepping away, she swiped at a tear rolling down her cheek. "Do you know when?"

"Not yet." Abigail chuckled. "I believe we'd marry tomorrow if Quinn could arrange it."

"Just like a man. They wait forever to ask you to marry them, then want to get it done as soon as possible. Jake was the same. When will you let everyone know?"

Mouth twisting, she shook her head. "I hadn't thought about it."

Beth tapped a finger against her lips. "Is he serious about having the ceremony soon?"

"I'm sure he is. It doesn't have to be anything fancy. We'll invite his parents and mine. They'll need time to get someone to take over their work while they're gone. Especially Quinn's folks." Abigail felt Rowdy nudge her ankle. Reaching down, she lifted him into her arms.

Beth grabbed a pad of paper and pen to start a list. "You'll need places for them to stay. Of course, your parents can stay with Jake and me. Invitations. A dress. Food for the reception. At the ranch, right?" She didn't wait for an answer. "Oh, and a minister." She glanced up at Abigail. "We can ask the one at the church most of us attend."

Abigail gave a slow nod, her mind going numb as she stared at the growing list. "Maybe we should elope."

"Not a chance, Abbie. You're having a real wedding, with a dress and flowers, and your friends and family. None of this slam-bam stuff. Now, what else?"

Beth's voice fell away as Abigail walked to the window, nuzzling Rowdy's soft fur. Late Sunday morning, and as expected, the ranch was quiet. Quinn and Logan would be driving over for lunch, which she'd already prepared and placed in the refrigerator.

"Abbie?" Beth's voice cut into her wandering thoughts. "Yes?"

"Are you going to have bridesmaids and Maid of Honor? If so, we need to plan for their dresses and flowers."

Sagging against the counter, she made a quick decision. "Will you be my Maid of Honor?"

Beth's smile broadened. "I'd love to stand beside you."

"That's all I need."

"So, no bridesmaids?"

"Right."

Beth continued to make notes. "I'm guessing Quinn will ask Jake to stand up for him."

"I'll have to ask Wyatt about having the reception here."

"How about I ask him, Abbie? You have enough to do. What about the ceremony?"

"What about it?"

"At the church or here?"

"Here, if the Bonners agree. I really should ask Quinn what he wants."

Beth waved a hand in the air. "As long as you're happy, he won't care. I'll ask Wyatt about the ceremony and the reception. You know, we could make this all happen in three to four weeks."

Abigail's eyes widened. "That soon?"

Walking to her, Beth draped an arm over her shoulders. "Honey, it's all up to you and Quinn. What I'm saying is we could have everything ready as soon as three or four weeks."

"Right." She blew out a breath. "He will be here for lunch. I'll talk to him."

"I'll meet you at the truck, Logan." Quinn grabbed the keys and his hat before opening the front door.

He came to an abrupt stop. A man he knew well stood on the porch, wearing an expression Quinn couldn't recall ever seeing.

"Pop. I didn't know you were coming." Quinn didn't move to give him the usual brief hug.

Wallace Sawyer glanced around, his gaze landing back on his son. "It was a last-minute decision. I'd like to talk to you...and Logan."

Quinn's eyes widened, his mouth twisting in disbelief. He wondered how Wallace had learned his sons had met. "How..." His voice trailed off as he motioned his father inside. "Do you want coffee or water?"

"Coffee would be good. I've been driving for a while."

"Black, right?"

"A little milk would be appreciated."

Giving a nod, Quinn set his hat and keys down as he walked into the kitchen. Adding a coffee pod to the machine, he set a cup underneath before rushing upstairs to intercept Logan.

He'd expected Jake and Beth to direct his brother to a bed in the bunkhouse with the other men. Instead, they'd insisted Logan stay in the house.

Meeting him in the hall, he held up a hand. "We have a visitor."

"Who?"

"Pop."

Logan's face went slack. "What? How?"

"I don't know. He's downstairs waiting for us. He knows you're here."

"Geez." Logan ran fingers through his hair. "Well, I guess the decision to confront him has been made for us."

"Guess so. I've made him a cup of coffee. Do you want some?"

Logan shook his head. "No, thanks. Let's get this started."

Downstairs, he grabbed three bottles of water before following Quinn into the living room.

"Hello, Pop."

Wallace turned from looking at the wall of photographs Beth had arranged. "Logan. It's been a while."

"Yeah, it has. How are you, Pop?"

"Oh, you know. Some days are better than others." Wallace took the bottle of water Logan offered, setting it down to take the cup of coffee from Quinn's outstretched hand.

Sitting down, he sipped the coffee for several minutes without looking at either of his sons. He didn't seem to be in a rush. Quinn and Logan lowered themselves onto the sofa, opened their water bottles, and waited.

They knew Wallace would talk when ready. He was a man who used words sparingly, never talking unless he had something to say. Shifting in the overstuffed chair, he took another sip of coffee. A full five minutes passed before he spoke.

"How'd you boys get together?"

Logan shot a look at Quinn, who nodded. "Mom told me about having an older brother. She gave me his name, and I tracked Quinn down a couple weeks ago."

Wallace gave a slow nod before meeting his oldest son's gaze. "My guess is you want to know why."

Quinn took a long draw on his water before setting the bottle down. "Yeah, Pop. That would've been my first question."

"And your second question?"

Quinn didn't hesitate. "Does Mom know about Claudia and Logan?"

His face expressionless, Wallace gave another slow nod. Standing, he took unhurried steps into the kitchen, placing his empty cup in the sink. Exhaling a deep breath, he leaned against the counter. Quinn could see their father from his position in the living room, though he made no move to join him.

"You want something to eat, Pop?"

"Nope. Already ate, Quinn."

"Fast food?"

"Yep. Mexican food an hour north of here."

Quinn shook his head. "Mom isn't going to be happy with you going off your diet."

Wallace scoffed at the warning. "Turkey, chicken, vegetables, fruit. And fish. A man could starve with that diet."

Logan rubbed his hands together. "You look fine to me."

"Not worth arguing about. Sally's doing what the doctor recommended. Can't squabble about her intentions. Guess the woman still wants me around."

Wallace pushed away from the counter, making his way back to the living room. His back straight as a lightning rod, he lowered his wiry frame into the same chair he'd abandoned several minutes earlier.

"How is Mom?"

Wallace didn't answer right away, though his eyes darkened at Quinn's question. "She's a good woman."

"You don't have to convince me. How's she doing?"

"Same as always."

"That doesn't tell me much, Pop. Is she healthy, happy?"

Wallace's gaze shifted to his boots. The same boots he'd worn for years, having them resoled when they'd wear down.

"She's healthy. Always has been."

"Is Mom still happy with life on the ranch?" Quinn didn't know why he needed to know. It seemed important.

"Don't know how happy she is. The smiles meant for me disappeared a long time ago."

Feeling his chest squeeze, Quinn closed his eyes and nodded, knowing what his father meant. "Then she does know about Logan and his mother."

Chapter Twenty-Four

Wallace's face drained of color as he remembered the day Sally confronted him about what she'd learned from a neighbor. Not one of their neighbors at the ranch. A woman who lived across the street from Claudia. Sally and Wallace had seen her several times on their trips to the leather shop in town.

His beautiful, vivacious wife, with a generous smile and heart, had been devastated. It seemed all the life had gone out of her when he'd confirmed his involvement with Claudia. The light in her eyes had dimmed, as had her glorious smile.

No matter how much he assured Sally he loved her and not Claudia, it did nothing to soothe the hurt he'd caused. He'd broken her spirit.

She'd stayed with him, but never recovered from his betrayal. It was hard to argue he held no love for Claudia, a woman he'd continued to see for several years before ending the affair.

"Yes, Sally knows about Claudia and Logan. She's known for a long time."

Logan leaned forward, resting his arms on his thighs. "Mother said I was four or five when you stopped visiting her. You only came by to spend time with me. Does that sound right?"

Wallace looked at his younger son, his eyes revealing the pain he felt. "About right."

"Is that when Mom learned about them?" Quinn asked.

"Yes. She learned about us from one of Claudia's neighbors."

"I was ten when Mom began to change. When you changed, Pop. Even at ten, I knew something was wrong."

Wallace stared at Quinn with a miserable, disbelieving glint in his eyes. "How?"

Quinn scrubbed a hand down his face, letting out a shaky breath. "Mom stopped laughing, stopped singing when she made dinner. She was just...different. Sad all the time." Standing, he walked to the large front window to stare at the barn. "You came in just before meals, ate, then left. Other than a few cursory words, you and Mom never spoke, stopped holding hands. You stopped being the parents I'd known all my life. I asked you what was going on, but you told me it wasn't my business. I thought one of you was sick."

The room grew silent for so long Quinn thought the conversation had ended. Walking back to the sofa, he grabbed his empty water bottle, intending to take it to the kitchen. He stopped when his father began to talk.

"I don't know how I let myself get caught up with Claudia. I loved your mother, Quinn. Still love her."

"You never loved my mother, did you?" It was the first time Logan had spoken for a long time.

Wallace shook his head. "No."

"And me?"

"You're my son, Logan."

Drumming fingers against the arm of the sofa, he forced himself to appear unaffected. "Unlike my mother, I'm an obligation."

"Your mother was an addiction, Logan. Other than Sally, I've never been good at showing my feelings." Shoving up, Wallace walked to his youngest son, placing a hand on his shoulder. "I care a great deal about you. Don't ever doubt that."

Quinn could see by the disappointment on Logan's face, his brother had hoped for more.

"How did you meet Claudia?" Quinn still didn't understand how his father, a man who professed to love his wife, allowed himself to get involved with another woman.

Wallace turned to look at Quinn. "She worked at the lumberyard. We ended up at the same diner for lunch. She invited me to join her." Sucking in a slow breath, he labored with the rest. "Young and beautiful, we ended up at her apartment."

Hands fisted at his sides, he looked between his sons. One born out of love. The other born out of lust. Neither ever received the attention from him they deserved. He'd been a failure as a husband and as a father.

"Did you regret it?" Quinn asked.

"Every day since meeting her." Wallace cast an apologetic look at his youngest son. "God help me, but I couldn't stay away from her. When I made up my mind to end it, she told me about being pregnant. I'd go by her place every few weeks to make sure she was all right. I was there when you were born, Logan. Afterward, I only visited to spend time with you."

Quinn stared at his father with a mix of pity and disgust. His stomach churned when he thought of his mother, how she'd changed so much after learning of her husband's actions.

"Did you tell Logan about Darlene?" Wallace asked.

"A little."

"Your mother found a school for her. We moved Darlene there a few weeks ago. The letters from the administrator say she's doing real well."

"That's good."

Wallace reached into his pocket to pull out an envelope. He handed it to Quinn. "From your mother." Picking up his hat, he walked to the front door. "It's time for me to head back."

Neither of his sons tried to convince him to stay. Wallace had talked more than Quinn could recall. He didn't know about Logan, but he would need time to let it settle in before seeing his father again. More than anything, he wanted to talk to his mother.

Walking their father to his truck, the brothers exchanged glances. They had a good deal to discuss.

Opening the driver's side door, Wallace turned to face them. "Maybe someday you'll be able to forgive me. Maybe I'll even be able to forgive myself."

"It's not our forgiveness you need, Pop." Quinn took a small step forward. "You need to do whatever it takes to return the smile to Mom's face."

Quinn and Logan waited until their father's truck rounded the bend in the road before going back inside. Quinn held the envelope, while Logan had both hands shoved into the pockets of his jeans. Both stared at the ground, woodenly placing one booted foot in front of the other.

The living room had a different feel to it after the conversation with their father. Not unwelcoming or eerie, but different.

Logan sat down, draping an arm over the back of the sofa. "Tell me more about Darlene. Why does she need a special school?"

Quinn chose to pace the room as he spoke. "You already know she's four years younger than me, so a couple years older than you. Darlene is a simple person. Loving but fragile. The doctors have told Pop and Mom she's intellectually impaired. To look at her, she's the same as everyone else. If you talk to her for a few minutes, you'd hear nothing strange. Carrying on a longer conversation is different. That's when her impairment is noticeable. Mom's been trying to locate an affordable school for her. Guess she finally found one."

"I'd like to meet her. When the time is right, that is. I doubt your mother would want to be in the same room with me. At least not for a long time."

Logan stared out the window while Quinn continued to pace.

"I have to get out of here." Quinn picked up his hat and keys.

"Where are you headed?"

"I don't know. All I know is I have to clear my head."

Unaware he'd slammed the front door on his way out, Quinn rushed down the steps to his truck. He didn't recall his intention to have lunch with Abigail when he passed Whistle Rock Ranch. His thoughts were consumed with his father. Rather, what his father's actions had done to his wife and son. He thanked God Darlene would never understand the depth of their father's betrayal. This was an instance when her impairment was a blessing.

Turning onto the highway, he drove south, slowing through Brilliance, then picking up speed as he continued past the city limits. He'd been south of town one time, and hadn't driven far. That trip had been his attempt to get to know the area.

Today, he drove to put his father's confession into a context Quinn could accept. Or if not accept, live with. He wondered how his mother lived with her husband's betrayal. Why had she chosen to stay?

The answer was simple. She stayed for Darlene.

Seeing the sign for a state park up ahead, he took the turnoff, weaving his way to an empty camping spot. Parking, he tugged his mother's letter from a pocket. Unfolding it, he began to read.

My Dearest Quinn,

This will be a quick note, as your father is ready to leave. He knows you and your half-brother have met and are at a ranch down south.

I want you to know I forgave your father a long time ago for his time with Claudia. I've found forgiving was easier than forgetting. I'm still hopeful trusting him again will happen. As time goes by, my hope has diminished. Though I've forgiven him, I simply haven't been able to put what happened behind me.

I've found a wonderful school for Darlene. It's for people who are at least twenty and need more training if they desire to live on their own. I've used some of the money from your grandfather's estate to purchase a small house close to the school. Your father knows about this and has accepted I'll be moving there within the next month.

Once settled, I'll send you the address. My phone number remains the same.

You need to remember I love you, Quinn. No matter what the future holds for your father and me, my love for you and Darlene will never change.

My love,
Mom

Quinn read the note a second time, frustrated at the tears pooling in his eyes. None of the irritation was directed toward his mother. These feelings were due to his father's actions and how they'd affected his wife and son.

He didn't blame his mother for moving off the ranch. Maybe time away from each other would benefit her relationship with Wallace. One other piece of information stuck with him.

His mother had forgiven her husband. Quinn would need to find a way to do the same.

Pulling out his phone, he saw it had no bars. He needed to find a spot where there'd be good reception.

Driving out of the park, he turned north. The contents of the note still played in his mind. What struck him was his mother's quiet grace over the years since learning of Wallace's deception. She might not have found happiness. What she found was a way to forgive. He could do no less.

Checking his phone, he continued to a pull-out. Parking off the highway, he hit a number.

"Hi, Mom. It's Quinn."

Chapter Twenty-Five

Abigail wiped down the counters, glad the lunch crowd had left. More ranch hands had stayed at the ranch than normal on a Sunday, compelling her to prepare more sandwiches and Nacho's famous potato salad.

She'd been tempted to call Quinn, deciding against it. Standing her up wasn't his style. Something had come up to keep him away, she was sure of it. Logan hadn't shown up, either. Whatever had kept Quinn from lunch also kept Logan away.

"Are you good for handling dinner tonight?" Beth stopped beside her, a purse slung over one shoulder.

"I am. Are you going out?"

"Jake's taking me to the barbecue place he likes. Anywhere works for me." She offered a tired smile. "See you tomorrow."

"Have a good time." Abigail leaned against the counter, watching Beth leave.

She checked the time. Three o'clock and no word from Quinn. Maybe he'd show up for dinner.

Ready for another shower, she hung up her apron before turning toward her apartment. She came to an abrupt stop when her name was called.

"Good afternoon, Abigail."

"Hello, Jonah." Her attention shifted to a woman standing beside him.

"Abigail, this is Viviana Candelario. Viviana, Abigail Kelman."

The women exchanged greetings before Jonah continued. "Viviana is the woman I mentioned to you. She owns a gift basket business."

Abigail smiled at Viviana. "I remember. You're considering leasing one of the warehouses."

"That's right. Jonah showed me the warehouse this morning. He's now giving me a tour of the ranch. It's quite impressive."

"I thought the same when accepting the position here."

"What is it you do, Abigail?"

"I'm the assistant cook."

"Don't let the title fool you," Jonah said. "Abbie and the chef, Beth, are quite talented. Our family and ranch hands eat extremely well. If you have time, we'll eat dinner here before I drive you back to the bed and breakfast."

"Dinner here would be fine, Jonah." Viviana shifted to look at Abigail. "I'll look forward to it."

It was just before dinner when Quinn walked into the kitchen. Spotting Abigail finalizing the trays of food, he closed the distance between them. She didn't hear his approach, her focus on the upcoming dinner. Sensing someone behind her, she glanced over a shoulder.

"Hey," she whispered.

"Hey, yourself. I heard Jake was taking Beth to dinner. Do you need help?" He walked to Rowdy's pen. Bending down, he scooped the puppy into his arms.

"Thanks, but I have everything ready for when the ranch hands arrive."

"At least I can help carry out the trays." Which he did, greeting the people he knew as they entered.

Quinn continued helping after everyone left. When the last plate had been set in the dishwasher, he dried his hands and faced her.

"Sorry about lunch. Something came up."

Removing her apron, she set it on a hook. "Must've been important."

"Yeah, it was."

She waited for him to explain. When he didn't, she pulled down a couple plates for their dinner. He watched her fill both.

"We can eat in the kitchen or my apartment."

He looked around as if verifying they were alone. "Here is fine." He set Rowdy back into his pen.

Abigail didn't press him to explain, letting Quinn choose when to bring it up again. He did about halfway through their dinner.

"My father showed up."

"What? You mean he didn't call or anything?"

"No. I answered a knock on the door and there he stood."

"Were you and Logan together?"

"Yeah."

"What did he say?"

"He wasn't surprised to see us together. Someone, I don't know who, tipped him off that Logan was here."

Quinn ate a couple more bites before setting his fork down. "Mom has known about Logan for a long time." Leaning back in the chair, he massaged the back of his neck. "Pop explained it all." He pulled his mother's letter from a pocket, holding it out to Abigail. "Mom had him deliver this to me."

She read the short note twice before handing it back to him. "I am so sad for her. For both of them."

Rubbing his chin, he placed his mother's letter back in his pocket. "I don't know what this means for their marriage. I called her earlier. We didn't talk about Logan, or our engagement."

"It can't be good with her moving into a separate house. Maybe you should drive up there?"

"I was thinking the same. We don't have a game next Saturday, so probably next weekend. Any chance you'd like to go with me?"

"Are you sure you want me to tag along?"

A small smile appeared. Picking up her left hand, he touched the engagement ring. "Definitely. It would be a great time to announce our engagement to her."

Feeling her face heat, she returned his smile. "I'll talk to Beth tomorrow."

The drive north took a little more than three hours, giving Quinn and Abigail time to talk. They had a great deal to discuss. Rowdy sat in her lap the entire time, sleeping when not staring at her or Quinn.

Abigail had been at the Sawyer ranch twice when they first dated. Quinn's father had built the ranch house and barn with little help. Over time, he'd added more space and wrapped the front porch around two sides of the home.

The years hadn't been kind to the wood structure. Running the ranch with one other man left little time to keep up on chores such as painting and repairs.

Holding Rowdy, she didn't know what to expect when Quinn opened the door for her. Original furniture had aged along with the house, as had the draperies, and wallpaper in the entry. Regardless, Quinn's mother had kept the inside spotless.

"Mom. Are you here?"

Seconds passed before a woman wearing an apron with her hair in a ponytail came rushing from another room. She wore a huge smile, her eyes glinting in delight.

"Quinn. What a wonderful surprise!"

He picked her up, giving her a hug. Laughing, she slapped his shoulder.

"Put me down, silly." Her words were clear, though said with a smile.

Abigail knew Sally Sawyer was in her fifties. Her brown ponytail had touches of gray, but her skin and figure were that of a much younger woman.

"I decided to surprise you, Mom. You remember Abbie, right?"

"Of course, I remember her. And who do we have here." Sally ran a hand over Rowdy's head and back.

"This is Rowdy."

"He's a cutie. It's good to see you, Abbie. Come into the kitchen and I'll fix you something to eat."

"We're good for now, Mom."

"Nonsense." She took Abigail's arm, threading hers through it on the way to the kitchen.

Pulling her arm free, she made them each a cup of coffee before setting ingredients for sandwiches on the counter. Placing them before Quinn and Abigail, she sat down.

"What brings the two of you all the way up here?"

Sipping his coffee, Quinn glanced at Abigail. "You already know Pop visited me a few days ago?"

She set her arms on the table. "Yes. I believe he was confirming you and Logan had met."

"I tend to agree. Logan is working with me at Jake Kelman's ranch. We were together when Pop arrived." Quinn took a bite of his sandwich.

Sally gave a considering nod. "He told me little about how it went."

The delicious sandwich tasted bitter in his mouth. "He, uh, talked about Logan and his mother."

"I guessed this was the purpose of him being gone for a full day. So now you know." The glint had gone out of her eyes.

"Logan had explained quite a bit before Pop arrived." Setting the sandwich down, he reached over, placing his hand over his mother's. "I wanted to take him apart for what he did to you."

Her lips pinched together. "It's been a long time."

"I doubt the pain ever goes away."

Reaching up, she swiped a tear threatening to fall. "I've forgiven Wallace, but have had a hard time putting it all behind me." She let out a shaky breath.

"I have some good news for you."

"Oh?" She swiped under her eyes a second time while forcing a weak smile.

He reached for Abigail's left hand, holding it up to display the engagement ring. "Abbie has agreed to marry me."

"Oh, my gosh, Quinn. That is such wonderful news." Standing, she hugged Abigail, then her son. "When? Where?"

"As soon as we can arrange it," Abigail answered. "We plan to have it at Whistle Rock Ranch. The Bonners have offered to host the reception. Actually, they insisted on hosting it."

"I'll take care of securing a place for you and Pop to stay while you're there."

Sally stared at her hands. "Let me know the date, and I'll reserve rooms for us."

Quinn shot a look at Abigail to see if she'd picked up on the plural of room. She gave an almost imperceptible nod.

"I'll get names of places as soon as Abbie and I decide on a date."

Sally looked at Abigail. "I'd like to help. Driving down early isn't a problem. I have my own car."

"I'd love to have your help. I'll speak with Margie and Daisy Bonner when we get back to the ranch."

"Wonderful. Now, tell me about Logan."

"Are you sure you want to talk about him, Mom?"

"Your father won't tell me anything about his other son. I'm curious about him. It must've been hard for him."

Pulling out his phone, Quinn selected a picture Beth had taken of him and Logan. He held the phone out to his mother. "This is a picture a friend took a couple weeks ago."

Sally studied it for several seconds. "You and Logan have many of the same features. Your eye color is almost identical to his, and both of you have dark blond hair." Clearing her throat, she handed the phone back to Quinn. "You and Logan look like Wallace."

"Several people have said the same."

"I suppose he'll be at the wedding."

"If it would be too uncomfortable for you, Mom, I'll ask him not to attend."

"No, Quinn. I'll be fine. I always knew the day would come when I'd meet him. Your wedding will be the perfect place." Shoving away from the table, she stood. "You should hunt down your father. He's working in the northern pasture. Fixing fences, I believe. Take your truck. It will be faster."

"We could wait here with you until he returns, Mom."

"No, you go ahead. Will you be spending the night? Abbie can stay in Darlene's room."

Quinn and Abigail had discussed spending the night if his mother offered. Deciding to be open to the idea, each had packed a few items.

"We'd love to spend the night, Mrs. Sawyer," Abigail answered.

In a spontaneous action Quinn hadn't seen for many years, Sally pulled Abigail into a hug, before doing the same with Quinn.

"I am so happy you've come. Now, go find Wallace. I'm certain he'll be glad to see you."

Chapter Twenty-Six

Wallace ran a strand of new wire between one post and the next, using a tool to tighten the wire. He worked alone. His latest ranch hand had taken what was to be a short vacation to visit relatives in South Dakota. One week had stretched to two, then three, before Wallace realized the man wasn't going to return the messages he'd left. He figured the ranch hand never planned to return.

Finishing the task, he surveyed what was left. Figuring it would take another two hours, he reached down for the jug of water, taking a long swallow. This was when he noticed the truck coming toward him.

Swiping an arm across his forehead, he studied the truck as it came closer. His throat tightened when he recognized the driver, but not the passenger, though he could tell it was a woman.

Wallace tugged off his gloves, tucking them into a back pocket. His gaze never left the truck as Quinn waved a hand out the window and parked. Setting the jug down, he closed the distance between them.

"Hey, Pop." Quinn held out his hand, which his father accepted.

"Quinn. Didn't know you were coming." His attention moved to the woman who joined them.

"Pop, do you remember Abbie Kelman?"

"Yes." Wallace held out his hand, grasping hers.

"Hello, Mr. Sawyer. It's been a while."

"Call me Wallace." He looked back at Quinn. "What brings you up here?"

Grabbing Abigail's hand, he held it up to show the ring. "We're planning to marry soon. I wanted to let you and Mom know in person. We'd like you to be at the wedding."

"Let us know when. Even if I can't make it, your mother will be there."

"We hope both of you can attend, Wallace."

"It all depends on what needs to be done. The ranch hand left, so I've got to find someone else."

Quinn studied his father's face, seeing complete indifference. Unless something changed, he didn't believe Wallace would make the drive with Sally.

"You know, Pop, the wedding is important to me and Abbie. I've asked nothing of you or Mom since graduating from high school. When you've called needing help, I've dropped whatever I was doing to help out. It never mattered what it was or how much time it would take. I was there for you." Quinn saw the discomfort on his father's face, deciding to continue. "I want you to think about that when you make a decision to stay here or attend the wedding with Mom."

Rowdy bounded around the kitchen while Abigail and Sally finished preparing dinner. He'd been loose for over an hour, providing occasional laughter at the end of what had been an interesting day.

Quinn's mother had asked her to season the roast chicken and vegetables before sliding them into the oven. Removing them to check doneness an hour later, Sally smiled at the incredible aroma.

"This is going to be incredible. It needs a few more minutes." Sally slid the roast chicken back into the oven. "What will you do about your job at the ranch, Abbie?"

"No change. Quinn will continue working for Jake and I'll remain in the kitchen at Whistle Rock. We'll live in the new foreman's house Jake is building for Quinn."

"Sounds perfect." Sally's wistful voice caught Abigail's attention.

"It is. Um, this probably isn't my business, but Quinn told me you bought a house and are leaving the ranch."

"Yes. I wrote about the move in the letter Wallace gave Quinn. It's a few blocks from Darlene's school." Sally knelt down to play with Rowdy. "He is just too cute, Abbie."

Abbie stood a few feet away, watching the older woman and Rowdy. "Will you and Wallace divorce?"

Sally stood, taking a while to answer. "Not unless he wants to. I'm hoping putting space between us might provide a clear perspective. For me, not Wallace. I'm the one having difficulty putting the past behind me." Walking to a hutch, she pulled out dishes before letting out a deep sigh. "We've had our ups and downs over the years. Right now, we seem to be in a deep trough that I can't seem to claw out of. There's a therapist close to where I bought the house. I've already scheduled two meetings. It's what I can do for now."

Abigail felt an acute sadness roll through her. It was apparent Wallace and Sally loved each other. Hearing their story provided an intense lesson in love. Trust, once lost, was almost impossible to regain.

"Hey. I smell something wonderful." Quinn's voice brought a smile to her face. Hearing boots on the hardwood floor, she met him in the living room.

"Did you finish repairing fences?"

"All done. Pop is right behind me." He lowered his voice. "How's Mom?"

"She's determined to move to the new house. There's a therapist close by. She already has a couple appointments scheduled."

He shot a look toward the kitchen. "I sure hope it helps get them back together."

"Maybe the move is the best for both of them. I certainly hope it is."

Several weeks later...

"Why does the dress feel tighter than it did when I bought it?" Abigail tugged at the zipper, her lips twisted in concentration. "It's only been three weeks since I purchased it."

Daisy Bonner laughed, as did Lily Cardoza. "The same happened to us," Daisy answered. "That's why you try it on again before the wedding. Gives us time to make alterations."

"Right. What else needs to be done?" Abigail asked as she studied the dress in the mirror Daisy had brought with her.

Lily grabbed a piece of paper from a counter in the lodge's kitchen. "Not much. The flowers have been ordered, the menu is set, almost all the guests have already confirmed attendance, the music has been selected, and Lydia at the bakery has agreed to prepare the wedding cake. We haven't heard from Quinn's parents."

"I know." Abigail slid out of the dress. "I'll ask Quinn if he's heard from them."

She'd been asking every day for the last two weeks. The answer had always been the same. He'd left a message and neither had returned it.

"I've reserved a room for them at the bed and breakfast at the south end of town. The owner, Britt Holmes, said I can cancel up to forty-eight hours in advance."

Beth set down the sample centerpiece she'd been arranging for the tables. "That's good of Britt, Abbie. She usually requires at least a week notice."

"I'm hoping we'll still hear from them." Abigail couldn't believe neither of them would attend their son's wedding.

Quinn had received a short note a week after they left the ranch, saying she'd moved into the house. He and Abigail were surprised at the speed of her move. Sally didn't explain the reason, and Quinn wasn't comfortable asking Wallace.

"I'd be surprised if they didn't attend." Lily made a few more notes on the list before setting it aside. "All the ranch hands will be there, as will several people from town."

"Except for Lydia, I don't recall inviting anyone from town."

"Margie added several names." Daisy mentioned her mother-in-law. "I didn't think you'd mind."

"I don't. Afterall, she and Anson are hosting the reception. Quinn and I are grateful for their generosity. I can't believe the wedding is just two weeks away." Abigail sat down, her mind drifting back to the visit with Quinn's parents.

Recalling the yearning in Sally's words, she was thankful her own parents seemed to have a secure relationship. They'd confirmed their attendance at the wedding the same day her mother had received the invitation. She'd made a reservation for them at the same bed and breakfast.

"Don't fret, Abbie." Beth placed a hand on her shoulder. "You have a horde of experienced women helping you. All you'll have to do is show up on your wedding day."

Abbie looked up at her friend and boss. "You make it sound so easy."

"It is what you make of it," Lily interjected. "Isn't that what you told me, Daisy?"

"I did, and your wedding went off perfectly."

Lily nodded. "You're right." She shifted to look at Abigail. "Yours is going to be perfect, also. Just relax and let us do the hard work."

"It doesn't sound so easy to me." Abigail stood to pick up Rowdy, who'd fallen asleep at her feet.

Daisy laughed. "It's common to be stressed. Just don't let it cause you to lose sleep."

Abigail told herself to relax several times as she ate dinner that night with Quinn. He'd waited until the Whistle Rock Ranch people had finished before joining her in the kitchen.

"Relax?" Quinn took a bite of the best beef stew he'd ever tasted, cocking his head to the side.

"Did I say that out loud?"

Chuckling, he nodded. "Yes. More than once."

"Sorry."

"You're not worried about the wedding, are you? Jake told me you have a group of semi-professionals handling it for us."

She smiled at the label Quinn had given the women. "Semi-professionals is perfect."

"How are the plans going?"

"Fine. We still haven't heard anything from your parents."

Quinn considered this as he chewed on another bite of stew. "Pop knows how much I want them here."

"I can't imagine your mother not being here. Maybe she thinks we know she's coming."

"If we don't hear anything by tomorrow, I'll call her." He stabbed a thick piece of beef, staring at his fork for several seconds. "She'll be driving by herself. I can't remember Mom ever venturing this far from home alone." Setting his fork down, he stood, pacing to the refrigerator for another bottle of water. Removing the cap, he drank half the contents. "Maybe I should drive up there."

"To do what?"

"Drive her down."

"We don't even know if she's able to be here."

"Trust me. Mom isn't going to miss her son's wedding."

"What about your father?"

Quinn shrugged. "He'll either be here or he won't. Pop knows how important this is to me." Leaning against a counter, he stared out the window.

Moving to stand beside him, she slid her arm through his. "Who would've thought how much their marital issues would affect our wedding."

Lowering his head, he kissed her. Straightening, he opened his mouth to speak when his phone buzzed, indicating a text message. Pulling it from a pocket, he read it, a smile appearing on his face.

[Mom]: I'll arrive two days before the wedding. Darlene is coming with me. Looking forward to being there and helping Abbie. Love you.

Handing it to Abigail, she read it, smiling along with him.

Epilogue

Quinn couldn't help chuckling as Abigail slipped a large bite of their wedding cake into his mouth. Chewing, he swallowed, looking for the glass of punch on the table. When he didn't see it, Abigail held hers out.

Abigail's turn came next. Quinn threatened with a piece as large as his, then relented, holding out a much smaller forkful. The guests clapped, then formed a line for their own slices.

Taking her hand, Quinn guided her across the room. The band the Bonners hired played a slow song. They watched the only couple dancing. Sally and Wallace Sawyer.

They'd been stunned when his parents arrived three days before the wedding with Darlene in the back seat. Wallace had held the door open for Sally, taking her hand the instant she set her feet on the ground.

Quinn had insisted they have dinner together the night they arrived. It was over roasted chicken his parents explained the turnaround in their marriage. The story wasn't long or complicated. Since then, you couldn't find one without the other.

Wallace had given her a week before showing up at the new place. It had been an emotional several hours as the two spoke, argued, and yelled. When morning came, Sally had agreed to return to the ranch. Wallace taking a chance had worked out.

"I know I've said this before, Quinn. It's wonderful about your parents. And how Sally had accepted Logan."

"It surprised me. Watching them dance, you'd never know they'd gone through years of suffering." Quinn took her hand. "Let's join them."

Less than a minute passed before several other couples danced around them. When the song changed to a faster number, more people walked onto the dance floor.

As he whirled Abigail around to the beat of the song, his gaze moved to Logan. His brother was talking with Aiden Winters, a man Quinn never thought he'd see again. He wondered if the man had stumbled onto their wedding or been invited by someone. Quinn couldn't think of a reason why it mattered, as long as Aiden had a good time.

The band changed back to a slow number, pulling Abigail close, he leaned down to whisper in her ear. "Do you think anyone would miss us if we left?"

Laughing, she shook her head. "I tend to believe they would notice us leaving."

"We could say Rowdy needs to be fed."

"Won't work, cowboy. Rowdy is with one of the ranch hands."

Rubbing her back with his hand, he let out a sigh. "There must be something."

"It's called staying with our guests until an appropriate time to leave."

"Mrs. Sawyer?"

"Yes?"

"You aren't much fun." He winked at her.

Laughing again, she kissed his cheek as they made another turn around the dance floor.

"What do you know about Sam?" Quinn asked.

She drew back enough to look into his eyes. "Are you talking about Samantha Miller, the ranch hand? Gosh, I haven't thought about it. Why?"

"Logan's mentioned her several times. They're also dancing together."

"Quinn, a lot of people dance together."

When the song ended, he escorted her to a spot near the refreshments. "What do you know about her?"

"My understanding is that Trace Griffin referred her to Virgil. He knew her from his rodeo days. I don't think she's ever been married. Everyone likes and respects her. Oh, and I've heard Virgil say she's a hard worker. Is that enough?"

Chuckling, he nodded. "Yeah."

They stood next to each other, holding each other's hand, watching their guests dance and talk. Across the room, he saw Logan talking to Sam.

"You know, Quinn, you can't stop Logan from asking Sam out."

"Who said anything about Logan dating Sam?"

Laughing once more, she squeezed her husband's hand. "Quinn Sawyer, you aren't the most subtle man around. I love you anyway."

He met a gaze filled with amusement, thoughts of Logan and Sam forgotten. Quinn smiled at the woman who was now his wife.

"I'd certainly hope so, Mrs. Sawyer."

Learn about upcoming books in **The Cowboys of Whistle Rock Ranch** series at shirleendavies.com.

Enjoy the Whistle Rock cowboys? You might want to read **Macklins of Whiskey Bend**.

If you want to keep current on all my preorders, new releases, and other happenings, sign up for my newsletter at http://www.shirleendavies.com/contact-me.html

A Note from Shirleen

Thank you for reading **The Cowboy's Surprise Reunion**!

Leave a Review! If you enjoyed the, please consider posting a short review and telling your friends. Word of mouth is an author's best friend and much appreciated.

I care about quality, so if you find something in error, please contact me via email at **shirleen@shirleendavies.com**

Books by Shirleen Davies

Contemporary Western Romance Series

MacLarens of Fire Mountain

Second Summer, Book One
Hard Landing, Book Two
One More Day, Book Three
All Your Nights, Book Four
Always Love You, Book Five
Hearts Don't Lie, Book Six
No Getting Over You, Book Seven
'Til the Sun Comes Up, Book Eight
Foolish Heart, Book Nine

Macklins of Whiskey Bend

Thorn, Book One
Del, Book Two
Boone, Book Three
Kell, Book Four
Zane, Book Five
Josh, Book Six, Coming Next in the Series!

Cowboys of Whistle Rock Ranch

The Cowboy's Road Home, Book One
The Cowboy's False Start, Book Two
The Cowboy's Second Chance Family, Book Three
The Cowboy's Final Ride, Book Four
The Cowboy's Surprise Reunion, Book Five
The Cowboy's Counterfeit Fiancée, Book Six, Coming
Next in the Series!

Historical Western Romance Series
Redemption Mountain

Redemption's Edge, Book One
Wildfire Creek, Book Two
Sunrise Ridge, Book Three
Dixie Moon, Book Four
Survivor Pass, Book Five
Promise Trail, Book Six
Deep River, Book Seven
Courage Canyon, Book Eight
Forsaken Falls, Book Nine
Solitude Gorge, Book Ten
Rogue Rapids, Book Eleven
Angel Peak, Book Twelve
Restless Wind, Book Thirteen
Storm Summit, Book Fourteen
Mystery Mesa, Book Fifteen

Thunder Valley, Book Sixteen
A Very Splendor Christmas, Holiday Novella, Book Seventeen
Paradise Point, Book Eighteen,
Silent Sunset, Book Nineteen
Rocky Basin, Book Twenty
Captive Dawn, Book Twenty-One
Whisper Lake, Book Twenty-Two, Coming Next in the Series!

MacLarens of Fire Mountain

Tougher than the Rest, Book One
Faster than the Rest, Book Two
Harder than the Rest, Book Three
Stronger than the Rest, Book Four
Deadlier than the Rest, Book Five
Wilder than the Rest, Book Six

MacLarens of Boundary Mountain

Colin's Quest, Book One,
Brodie's Gamble, Book Two
Quinn's Honor, Book Three
Sam's Legacy, Book Four
Heather's Choice, Book Five
Nate's Destiny, Book Six
Blaine's Wager, Book Seven
Fletcher's Pride, Book Eight
Bay's Desire, Book Nine

Cam's Hope, Book Ten

Romantic Suspense

Eternal Brethren, Military Romantic Suspense

Steadfast, Book One
Shattered, Book Two
Haunted, Book Three
Untamed, Book Four
Devoted, Book Five
Faithful, Book Six
Exposed, Book Seven
Undaunted, Book Eight
Resolute, Book Nine
Unspoken, Book Ten
Defiant, Book Eleven

Peregrine Bay, Romantic Suspense

Reclaiming Love, Book One
Our Kind of Love, Book Two

Find all of my books at:
https://www.shirleendavies.com/books.html

About Shirleen

Shirleen Davies writes romance—historical and contemporary western romance, and romantic suspense. She grew up in Southern California, attended Oregon State University, and has degrees from San Diego State University and the University of Maryland. During the day she provides consulting services to small and mid-sized businesses. But her real passion is writing emotionally charged stories of flawed people who find redemption through love and acceptance. She now lives with her husband in a beautiful town in northern Arizona.

I love to hear from my readers!

Send me an email: shirleen@shirleendavies.com
Visit my Website: https://www.shirleendavies.com/
Sign up to be notified of New Releases:
https://www.shirleendavies.com/contact/
Follow me on Amazon:
http://www.amazon.com/author/shirleendavies
Follow me on BookBub:
https://www.bookbub.com/authors/shirleen-davies

Other ways to connect with me:

Facebook Author Page:
http://www.facebook.com/shirleendaviesauthor
Pinterest: http://pinterest.com/shirleendavies

Instagram:
https://www.instagram.com/shirleendavies_author/
TikTok: shirleendavies_author
Twitter: www.twitter.com/shirleendavies

Avalanche Ranch Press, LLC
PO Box 12618
Prescott, AZ 86304

Made in the USA
Middletown, DE
12 February 2024

49618201R00133